The 13
(Ashi-niswi)

Lorin R. Robinson

Open Books

Published by Open Books

Copyright © 2018 by Lorin R. Robinson

ISBN-13: 978-1948598071

For historian Dr. Walker D. Wyman (1907-1999),
source of the idea for *The 13*

The 13

READER REVIEWS

"An engrossing trip through the rocks and waters of the Anishinaabe world long before white culture disrupted the Native American way of life. Thirteen teenage boys take us on a life and death quest for honor pitted against the enemy Dakota and the unrelenting turns of the natural world. What price are they willing to pay?" (Cynthia Bend)

"An enthralling story from 'a time before time' that engages readers, stirs their compassion and pulls at their heartstrings. This finely woven and powerful Ojibwe tale is riveting and you will not put it down." (Kacie Bauzon)

"This story is a believable narrative about conflict, honor, decision-making and the duty of an individual to self, tribe and family that should engross all readers." (Tracy O'Connell)

"A masterpiece. I was captivated. Totally. I could not put it down. Extremely well told, the detail caused me to see the landscape, the people, the battles. The author mirrored native stories in a native way— through the mind, heart and gut." (Robert Schepens)

"I was surprised by how much I enjoyed this book. It was a quick read and I appreciated that the story wasn't drawn out or overdone. I kept on thinking about the book the entire next day and rethinking what I had read." (Eunice Peng)

An exciting page-turner. As old as the story may be, it has relevance for the international conflicts in the news today, which often seem to be a matter of honor for some world leaders. A highly recommended read." (Tom Spradley)

"I loved this story and couldn't put it down. The story is engrossing, but I think it will not appeal to everyone. The violence is difficult to read but necessary; it is not gratuitous." (Judith Burns Schuster)

Preface

Before white men, life
Was a circle, unbroken,
In silent forests.

It was a time before time.

The People of the Lake, of *Gichigami*, reckoned its passing by counting the seasons: *biboon*, winter, time of bone-cracking cold, of trapping, of hunger; *ziigwan,* spring, time of the Earth's rebirth, of flowing maple sap, of stripping birches; *niibin*, summer, time of plenty, of play, of planting maize, beans and squash; *dagwasagin*, fall, time of gathering rice, of harvesting, of preparing for the coming of *biboon*.

The *Anishinaabe*, or *Ojibwe* as they would be named much later by French fur traders, had lived on the shores of Gichigami, Lake Superior, almost since before memory. Only the old stories remained, told and retold at the gatherings each spring and fall to explain how The People came to this place.

According to the stories, the Anishinaabe originally lived close by the Great Salt Water near the Gulf of St. Lawrence. About 1,000 years ago, it is said they were instructed by seven prophets to migrate following the sacred *miigis,* a white seashell known as the cowry, toward the west until they reached a place where, mysteriously, "food grew upon the water."

The Anishinaabe lived in a land of plenty. Many did not want to heed the prophets' call. According to oral traditions, many vowed to remain despite the prediction that pale-skinned people would arrive from across the water and destroy their way of life. Most were decimated centuries later when the white man arrived.

Those who accepted the wisdom of the prophesy began their migration sometime around 1000 A.D., stopping at seven places along the way. The miigis is said to have risen from water or sand at each location to indicate where to stop. Each new move was preceded by a vision.

The migrants traveled along the St. Lawrence River. The first stop, as prophesied, was a turtle-shaped island, probably near Montreal. In Anishinaabe culture, the turtle represents truth and is said to have been present at creation and carry the teachings of life on its back. Slow moving and meticulous, the turtle understands both the importance of a journey and the destination.

The second stop was the place of thunder water, Niagara Falls. The Detroit River was the third stopping place. Continued movement west led to the eastern shores of Lake Michigan and, eventually, north to Manitoulin Island near the confluence of

Lakes Huron, Michigan and Superior. A fifth stop was at the rapids joining Huron and Superior at what is now Sault St. Marie.

At that point the travelers split into two groups. One trekked north along Lake Superior; the other followed its southern shore to an island near today's Duluth, the sixth stopping place. Here, after decades, the northern travelers, who had circled the huge lake, rejoined the southern group.

The final vision—this of another turtle-shaped island—sent the reunited migrants some distance back east along Superior's southern shore. The island, with 12 others, is in a huge bay they called *Zhaagawaamikaang,* place of shallow waters. It is known today by the transliteration "Chequamegon."

Around this bay the Anishinaabe found the "food that grows on water," *manoomin,* wild rice, and an island they called *Mooningwanekaaning,* island of the yellow-shafted flicker. It became the center of their world and is now known as Madeline, the largest of the 13 Apostle Islands.

The migration took many generations and was fraught with danger. The migrants had to travel through lands settled long ago by others. Many died in the resulting conflicts. Many gave up the migration and assimilated with indigenous tribes met along the way.

But the migrants' most potent adversary was the *Dakota,* later renamed *Sioux* by the French, who fiercely resisted their spread into its territory—Upper

Wisconsin, Minnesota and the Lake Superior region. Gradually the Anishinaabe pushed them out of the northern woodlands and into the plains to the south.

This long-running and bloody conflict lies at the heart of the story of *The 13*.

The War Party

Aajim/Akiwenzil, Tell a Story/Old Man—Narrator of the story both as a 14-year-old and an ancient "grandfather."

Amik, Beaver, 16—A twin and jokester.

Animikil, Thunderer, 16—Aajim's elder brother.

Bimidoon, 15, Twisted Mouth—Aajim's cousin and a skilled tracker.

Gaagaagiw, Raven, 17—An orphan most comfortable communing with animals.

Gizhiibato, 16, Runs Fast—Tall and fleet of foot.

Inaabiwin, 16, Lightning—Son of the shaman.

Keeshegkoni, 16, Burning Fire—Instigator and leader of the war party.

Makwa, 15, Bear—Aajim's best friend.

Mangazide, 14, Big Feet—Small of stature despite his name.

Mikige, 17, Finds Things—A refugee from a decimated band.

Miscowaagosh, 17, Red Fox—Simple, but good natured.

Oshkagoojin, 16, New Moon—Amik's twin, also a jokester.

Prologue

It was the flying dream.

Akiwenzil could feel the wind ruffling his feathers as he flew slowly south, the woodlands below gradually thinning; the plains, the waiving grasslands of the enemy Dakota, spreading to the horizon. He knew where he was going. He didn't want to go. But his spirit guide, Giniw, golden eagle, could not be turned; would not let him awaken.

Smoke smudges in the distance. Soon a huge Dakota encampment spread beneath him bordering a large, bright-blue lake. Hundreds of cooking fires sent plumes of smoke rising like strings into the still morning air. He screamed to make his presence known. Some looked up, shielded their eyes against the low sun and marveled at the size of the majestic bird. The men coveted his tawny feathers for headdresses and ceremonial robes.

Giniw began circling over a large clearing in the center of the encampment. Wisely he stayed above bow and arrow range. Below a crowd had gathered in a large circle. The circle split and two groups of young men and boys, painted and dressed only in breechclouts, entered the ring from opposite sides. They carried weapons. The circle closed and the contestants spread around its inner rim.

An old man clothed in decorated deerskin and elaborate headdress stepped to the center. Akiwenzil could not hear his words. But he knew what they were. The chief signaled and two young men entered the ring from either side.

The contests were beginning.

Giniw screamed again. Among those contestants looking skyward to regard the soaring eagle, Akiwenzil saw his own young, frightened face—the face of Aajim.

The old man awoke with a gasp, his weak heart pounding in his chest. He lay quietly on the floor of the smoky *wiigiwaam* until he felt he was back in control of his body and senses. Someday, he thought, the dream will kill me.

He rose slowly, dropping his sleeping robe. He gently opened the stiff hide flap and, back bent, contorted his way into the gray of pre-dawn. So as not to wake the sleepers inside, he quietly replaced the door flap of the hut. He straightened slowly, stifling a gasp as the pain in his back radiated up his spine and down into his legs. The cold, early spring air assaulted his lungs. He hacked up phlegm, the price paid for sleeping in the hut's smoky interior. The cold made his rheumy eyes tear.

He wrapped the tattered hide robe around his shoulders and tottered into the foggy chill. The cold of the frozen ground penetrated his thin moccasins. As he neared the remains of the previous night's cooking fire, the black dog, sleeping on the now cold ashes, opened his one good eye and watched the old man's progress down the trail. He stood slowly, extended his front paws, arched his back and stretched—his long pink tongue lolling to one side.

The dog trotted ahead as he always did, stopping occasionally to check the old man's progress. Hurry, Akiwenzil, he seemed to say. He led them off the trail and a short way into the woods to their tree. The two of them made water, their streams steaming and mingling.

The dog led him back to the rocky path and down the hill. The trail switched-back several times, tall pines on the up slopes, their tops hidden in fog, their black roots clinging like claws to hold them to the hillsides. At each jog in the path the dog waited and looked back at Akiwenzil as if to say, come on old man, you get slower every day.

Once he took off into the underbrush as he sometimes did, ever hopeful of scaring up a hare, squirrel or raccoon still shaking off the effects of hibernation. Soon he was back on point. If disappointed by his fruitless foray, he kept it from the old man.

Even before rounding the final bend, Akiwenzil sensed his destination. There was the sound of waves lapping on a rocky shore, of the cracking, creaking of ice sheets as wave action fractured, rocked and rubbed them together. And then there it was. Gichigami. Great Water.

The lake spread to his left and right as far as his watery eyes could penetrate the ghostly fog that swirled slowly, softly into wispy shapes. He picked up the walking stick he always left propped against a boulder and descended the steep remainder of the path carefully, avoiding still frozen puddles in its crevasses. This is the hard part, he thought. Soon I will not be able to manage this short stretch. He stopped every few feet to catch his breath.

Once on the rocky beach, he walked slowly, wary of the uneven footing. Soon he approached his seat, a flat-oblong boulder nestled against the black trunk of a long-dead jack pine. The dog was waiting patiently, spread out at the foot of the rock, his stumpy tail thumping on the gravelly ground.

Leaning on his stick, the old man slowly lowered himself onto the cold slab. Ah, he thought as pain radiated from his back, sitting down is as bad as standing up. Leaning against the worn tree trunk, he closed his eyes and breathed deeply. The boulder's cold penetrated his thin robe, chilling his boney butt. How long have I been doing this he asked himself? As long as the band has been coming here to spend winter and spring. A *very* long time.

He slowly opened his eyes and looked east over the lake's tortured but receding ice pack. The sky was starting to lighten. Soon he would welcome *giizis*, the sun, and a new day. Soon there would be a little warmth to drive some of the chill from his bones.

Idly he looked northeast. Somewhere beyond his vision, about a half day's paddle, was Mooning-wanekaaning, the island destination of The People so long ago. It was there that, in the naming ceremony, he received his real name. He wasn't always known as Akiwenzil, Old Man. His given name was Aajim, Tell a Story. The name, bestowed by the medicine man after fasting, meditation and dreaming, was unusual and puzzled his parents and relatives. Names that seemed to predict a child's path were rare.

Akiwenzil smiled ruefully. He remembered how he hated his name as a child. Almost all the other boys were named for revered animals or objects in the natural world. He remembered boys from his youth—*Amik,* Beaver; *Makwa*, Bear and *Keeshegkoni*, Burning Fire. He also remembered how he actively refused to tell stories. Stubbornly, he would not allow the name to have any power over him.

He barked a laugh and shook his head. The dog, awakened from the hunting dream, looked up at him. How strange he thought, as he had many times before, that it was a story—the telling of a story—that had kept him alive long enough to become the oldest man known among the many bands living on the shores of Gichigami around the huge bay called

Zhaagawaamikaang, the place of shallow waters. Long enough to become Akiwenzil.

If it weren't for the story, he knew he would long ago have walked his bag of bones deep into the woods to die. He'd often imagined saying goodbye to the few family he had left, and, as useless old people do, disappear to become food for the worthy predators with whom they lived, or to decay and return to the Earth as all things must. It would be winter, he thought. He'd remove his robe, sit under a tree and freeze. The death would be quick and relatively painless—much less painful than living had become.

Perhaps his body would be taken by a *windigo*, the winter cannibal monster, and torn limb from limb. Perhaps *ma'iingan*, wolf, or *bizhiw,* lynx, would finish what was left. Would, as it is said, some of his spirit be ingested with his flesh? Would a little of him live on in his animal brothers? Or, as he thought more likely, would his remains simply become shit that melts into the ground with the thaw?

But The People would not let him die. He was a slave to the story. Since he had few teeth left in his head, his granddaughter happily chewed his food for him. She made his robes and moccasins and tended to him when he was sick. So he lived on—Aajim, Tell a Story.

His stomach rumbled. The cooking fires would soon be lit. But he ate little, partly because he was rarely very hungry; partly because food was in short supply this early in spring. It had been an unusually long and brutal winter. There had been no starvation. But he wanted others to have as much of the food as possible; food not contributed through any labor of his own.

The pink rim of the sun slowly rose above the horizon. It threw a rosy path of light across the undulating tumbled, jumbled ice pack. Ice crystals in banks of fog, now bathed in light, sparkled with tiny *nagweyaabiin,* rainbows. Akiwenzil watched the day begin. The *anangoog,* stars that ruled the night, slowly went to sleep, winking out as the crystalline bowl of sky lightened. The stars marking *Mishibizhii,* the great underwater panther, were slipping below the horizon as the sun drove him from the sky. But *Biboon Kenoni,* Winter Maker, was still high overhead—his belt and ax, his arms and legs still visible.

It was on a morning much as this, Akiwenzil remembered, that the story began. When he was a boy, the band's traditional wintering place here along the shores of Gichigami was much closer to the ever-changing border between the Anishinaabe and its ancient enemy, the Dakota. Gradually The People had expanded into traditional Dakota lands, leading to frequent bloodshed.

Akiwenzil closed his eyes and, as he had countless times before, remembered that morning in vivid detail as if it had been only yesterday. The story began at this very spot. Soon he would don his ceremonial robes and, in the dancing light of a huge bonfire at the Spring Gathering, again tell their story, the story of The 13, Ashi-niswi.

He sensed rather than saw someone approaching. A small figure slowly materialized from out of the haze, haloed by the sun. The boy stopped, politely waiting for an invitation. Akiwenzil patted the bench. It was *Debwe*, Tells Truth.

"You are up early, my young friend."

"Sleep was hard. My sister is sick. She coughed most of the night."

They sat in companionable silence.

"*Nimishoomish*, Grandfather, why is it that you come here almost every morning?"

"Ah," he said, "someone must see to it that the sun finds its way back to our sky. Someone must see to it that the stars go quietly to bed to stoke their fires for the next night."

Debwe thought. "Then you are the bringer of dawn?"

"No," Akiwenzil smiled. "I have very little to do with it. But that would be a good job for an old man, would it not? Bringer of dawn?"

"Then do you come here to remember the story?"

The boy is very perceptive, Akiwenzil thought. More inquisitive than the others. He has shown real interest in the story.

"Yes, perhaps I do. My memories are becoming ghost-like, wispy. They fade and, unless I bid them return, disappear. Thinking and talking about the story helps me remember. Would you like to speak of it again with me tonight?"

Debwe smiled his agreement.

"Now, don't you have the morning cooking fire to light? Off with you."

He watched him go.

The dog looked up and wondered when the old man would begin his journey back to the camp—and food. Hungry, he stood and headed up the trail. He wanted to be in time to get what scraps he could. He looked back once; the old man was motionless, staring out over the slowly undulating water. Mentally, the dog shrugged. He'd seen this before and knew it would be some time before the old man started back. The dog wouldn't wait.

Chapter I

The Raid

It was Aajim's job to light the morning cooking fire. As he slipped out of the wigwam into the cold, foggy dawn, he carried the hide bag containing dry grass and pine needles. In it he could feel the flint stones he would strike to spark the tinder into flame.

Hunger had awakened him earlier than usual. It had been a long and especially brutal winter. This was his fourteenth spring, so he'd had only limited experience with winters. But his father had talked of the difficulty hunting and trapping in the unusually deep snows and penetrating the thick ice for fishing. Food was in short supply and everyone was happy to see spring starting to break winter's icy grip.

He lifted the hide covering the woodpile and took an armful of twigs and small branches to the fire pit. He crouched, opened the bag and made a small mound of tinder. Close by, he placed twigs that he would use as soon as the tinder was alight. Now, he thought, I'll play my game. Every morning

1

he counted the number of strikes it took to light the tinder. The fewer the strikes, the better the day would be.

He counted. *Bezhig, niizh, niswi, niiwin, naanan....* This is not, he thought, going to be a very good day. On the sixth strike, a strong spark created a tiny flame. As he bent over to blow the tinder into life, he heard a few of the camp dogs also come to life with tentative growls and barks. The dog posted outside the neighboring hut was standing, looking intently at the foggy tree line on the other side of the encampment. His hackles were raised; his fangs barred.

Aajim followed his gaze but saw nothing. Could it be that his father and the others were returning from several days of hunting? Not likely, he thought. A returning hunting party would hail the camp from a distance so as not to alarm people by its sudden appearance.

He stood and peered into the gray forest beyond the camp. Then he saw it. Furtive movement between the trees. Sudden fear gripped him. Move, he told himself. As he stamped out the small fire at his feet, he shouted with all the force he could muster, "*MAWINAZH, MAWINAZH*, ATTACK!"

With the sounding of the alarm, Aajim could see camouflaged shapes of Dakota warriors materialize from the mist. He turned and ran to the hut, yelling as he went. Once inside he shook members of his family awake—his mother, older brother and two younger sisters. It took only a moment, but it seemed like forever until all scrambled from the rear entrance of the hut and ran with him into the nearby woods.

His older brother, *Animikil*, Thunderer, had the presence of mind to grab one of his father's war clubs. But he knew—as they all did—it would mean certain death to try to oppose the attackers. With most of the men gone, the camp didn't stand a chance.

Crouching, they ran into the nearby woods. Their mother, *Misajidamoo*, Gray Squirrel, led. Animikil stayed in the rear. He had the only weapon. They took a familiar and well-worn trail for some distance so their tracks would be less obvious. Then she led them into the bush and down a ravine.

Aajim doubted they would be followed. Judging from screams heard from the encampment, the raiders were busy killing and looting. They would probably hit and run. But why now? Raids this time of year were rare. The Dakota had been lucky most of the men were gone. If the band had been at full strength, the outcome would probably have been very different.

The bottom of the ravine was filled with fog. They splashed into the shallow stream that wound through it and, barefooted, ran through its icy waters. There had been no time to put on moccasins or their warm robes. Aajim's feet soon were numb, but he didn't complain. This was the best way not to leave tracks. Then Misajidamoo led them up a rocky embankment. Animikil erased their tracks with a fallen pine branch.

Aajim knew where they were going. He and his friends sometimes played in several small caves hidden in the undergrowth at the top of the ravine. Winded and cold, the five slipped into one of the caves. The walls were wet, the ceiling dripping. It stank of bear. They were lucky its recent inhabitant—hibernation over—and her new cubs had left the lair. The family barely fit. They huddled to share each other's body heat.

It was difficult to know how long they endured the cold and penetrating damp. Slowly the small cave mouth lightened as day began. Aajim, who was nearest to the entrance, uncoiled himself and crawled to the opening. He peered through the brush, looking up and down the stream below. Nothing. Gazing to the west he saw black smoke rising above the trees. They'd burned the camp. The slight prevailing northwest wind carried the greasy smell of burning hide.

Animikil joined him and slid past. "What do you see, little brother?"

As the eldest son and head of the family in their father's absence, he would make the decision when to return to camp. He crawled from the cave and pushed the undergrowth aside to get a better look. He lay quietly for a minute, looking, listening, smelling.

He twisted his head to look at Aajim. With a nod he indicated they would begin the journey back to camp.

The distance was not great—probably less than a mile. The family went slowly, staying off paths beaten by animals or humans. They stayed low; moved quietly. As they went, Aajim noticed a large patch of edible mushrooms that had just pushed up through pine needles and debris on the forest floor. They were spikey, their flesh convoluted, and a prized source of food in early spring. He made note of their location. He knew food could now be in short supply.

Their caution was justified. It was possible the Dakota would hunt in the woods surrounding the camp for those lucky enough to escape the initial attack. It was more likely, however, that the raiders had finished their ugly business, gathered up their spoils and headed west as quickly as they could, hoping to get well ahead of a war party bent on revenge, retribution.

Slowly approaching the tree line east of camp, they crawled as close as they dared, keeping themselves hidden in the bushes and brush. They lay among a profusion of white snow flowers, the first to push through the melting snows.

What they saw was worse than their worst imaginings. From their vantage point, the family could see bodies scattered in disarray around the encampment. Others, who looked unhurt, wandered among the dead or sat, dazed, by the bodies of friends or relatives. They, like Aajim's family, had probably escaped to the woods and avoided the massacre.

Aajim wondered how many had been saved by his early warning.

The Dakota had torched many of the huts. Since there was no fire in camp when the raid began, they must have taken time to build one so they could burn what they could. Remnants of their fire still smoked in the center of the camp. They were not very successful. The hide-covered wigwams were damp with the morning's dew. Some burned, but most only smoldered. In some cases, the wooden poles supporting the huts had burned, causing the hide coverings to collapse.

It appeared the communal hut where furs and hides were gathered over the winter and stored was the main target of the raiders. It had been pretty well cleaned out.

On Animikil's signal, they rose and walked into the nightmare that was their home. Aajim wondered if theirs was the only family left intact. Approaching the fire, he saw a large, elaborately decorated spear driven into the ground. Its eagle feathers fluttered in the breeze. Animikil said it was left by the Dakota to taunt them and to identify their attackers. It was a dare. Come and get us, it said.

Animikil, though he had only 16 summers,

seemed to take charge. He and his mother organized the living into groups to scour the camp and nearby woods for wounded or others in hiding. Aajim's young sisters, shocked, eyes as round as pebbles, seemed unable to move without his urging. He herded them to the remains of their partly-burned hut and, to give them something to do, ordered the two to rummage through its interior to look for food, clothing, tools or weapons that remained.

As the searchers spread out in the surrounding woods, Animikil organized others to carry or drag bodies to the center of the camp so they could be identified and a count taken. Others were sent to locate and stockpile food, hides and furs the raiders either missed or couldn't carry off.

The fire was rekindled to warm the living and wounded.

The assembled bodies, 14 of them, were a grizzly sight. Aajim had seen bodies of those killed in battle; bodies that had been brought back for burial. But they were warriors killed in combat. These were primarily the band's old men and women dragged from their huts in sleeping clothes. Among the dead also were two mothers whose children had been slaughtered with them.

Most had been killed by spear or ax. Some had been shot in the back with arrows as they fled. The attackers had pulled the arrows from their flesh. They were too valuable to be left behind. All the dead, including women and children, had been scalped.

Aajim knew that scalps of women and children were especially prized because they proved the raiders had dared to penetrate deep into enemy territory.

Two of Aajim's friends also lay dead with the others—*Misakakojish*, Badger; and *Bangli Omiimii*, Little Dove. Only yesterday the three and several others had gone to forage in the woods for mushrooms and to tap maple trees for their sap. They had also begun to identify likely birches that would later be stripped for their all-important bark.

The day had been bright and relatively warm. They had run through the woods, hidden from each other, laid in ambush, attacked and rolled good naturedly on the pine-needle carpeted forest floor. For a time he and Omiimii sat shyly together beside a rushing stream swollen by snow melt. The two were special friends, but nothing more. At the coming Spring Gathering, Omiimii would probably have been courted by young warriors from other bands.

Looking at her now, her exuberant life force stilled, her innocent beauty despoiled, a lump formed in Aajim's throat. I will not cry, he told himself. He had heard his father say: "Anishinaabe warriors do not waste their tears."

There would be revenge.

Chapter 2

THE MEN RETURN

IT WAS LATE IN THE DAY. Searchers had found three children hiding in the forest. Another of Aajim's friends had also been found—with an arrow in his thigh. He had lost a lot of blood but probably would survive.

The count of dead and living indicated that two of the band were missing—a young boy and a girl. Unless they were still hiding in the woods, it was likely they had been taken by the Dakota. They were the perfect age to be kidnapped and brought up as slaves. And they would be another sign of the bravery of the raiders.

Sick of sitting among the dead, Aajim decided to retrace his family's steps and harvest the mushrooms he had seen. On his way he made a short detour to visit the grave of his sister who had died two springs earlier at age three. His mother had named her *Opiche*, Robin, because the bird was the first thing she saw leaving the hut carrying her new-born. It would be Opiche until the formal naming ceremony. But the baby was frail, sickly and never able to travel. So she remained Opiche until her tiny body gave out.

Aajim stood before the grave. It would have been invisible except for the tree growing from its center. As was sometimes done, a sapling had been planted on the grave—a small tree that would soon be covered with delicate white and pink blooms—to mark its location and honor the deceased. Idly, he bent down to clear some brush and debris from the base of the sapling.

He put a hand flat on the ground for a moment to connect with his baby sister. He was glad she hadn't lived to experience this day of death. He pictured her remains a few feet beneath him, laid out with her feet facing west as was the custom—facing The Home After Death and the westward Road of Souls that would take her there. Arrayed around her were necessities for the journey—food, water, her tiny moccasins, her corn husk doll, her amber amulet.

Aajim stood, and, with one last look, turned and headed into the woods to try to find the mushrooms before dusk.

———————

He had almost finished plucking the tender fungi from the forest floor when he heard shouting from some distance. Finally. The men and older boys who had accompanied them were returning from the hunt.

Aajim rushed back to camp, careful not to jostle mushrooms from the woven reed basket he carried.

He arrived at the central clearing about the same time the men burst from the woods. It was clear they knew there had been trouble. No doubt they had seen or smelled smoke from some distance. Most were winded. They had probably been running for miles. Men carrying several deer slung on poles arrived last, exhausted.

Almost to a man they ran toward their own huts, or what remained of them. But all stopped when they came upon the row of the dead. It was impossible for Aajim to take in all that happened next. The few not finding dead parents, wives or children were soon surrounded by their families. Those who had suffered loss were consoled by the living.

Aajim ran to his father, *Mikinaak*, Snapping Turtle. He was walking down the line of the dead, looking for members of his family. Aajim spoke his name and Mikinaak looked up, obviously relieved. They embraced. Soon the other members of the family gathered around in a tight knot, everyone speaking at once. His father raised his hand for silence and hugged each family member.

But the joy on his face quickly fled as he surveyed the dead and the grief of other families.

One of the saddest sights Aajim would remember later was that of the *ogimaa*, chief, standing by himself at the edge of the fire looking at his dead wife. They had two daughters who had long ago married into other bands. He was now alone. He bent, scooped still warm ashes from the fire's edge, and, looking at his wife of so many seasons, smeared the black soot on his face, neck and arms. He then sat and cradled her ruined head in his lap. He had seemed to lapse into a trance and did not respond to offers of consolation.

———————

Preparing the dead was women's work. Even though night was approaching, the bodies were stripped and bathed. They were then dressed in the finest clothing that could be found in the devastated camp. At first light, parties would search the nearby forest for birch trees to strip of their white, flexible bark. The dead would be wrapped in the bark, seams sown with deer sinew. Birch bark was thought to be sacred and to protect the body from harm.

As the sky in the west burned blood red, the men gathered near the now large fire for a council meeting. The fire burned intensely, pine sap popping and sending sparks like fireflies skyward. Some of the women had butchered the fresh-killed deer and roasted choice pieces for the men. Several men had tried to get the chief to join them, but he was non-responsive and seemed incapacitated, lost in his grief.

No one knew how to start the meeting without the presence of Chief *Zegaanakwad,* Storm Cloud. There was no war chief. The band was small, totaling only about 90 members, and among the more peace-loving of the Anishinaabe in the region. Zegaanakwad had kept his people some distance from the constantly contested border with the Dakota to the west, hoping to avoid bloodshed such as this.

Inaabam, See in a Dream, passed a ceremonial pipe around the circle. He was the band's *shaman,* medicine man. He knew the meeting would be contentious. He hoped the sacred tobacco, shared by the men, would bring calm and wisdom to the deliberations. Each man exhaled puffs of the pungent smoke skyward to north, east, south and west to honor the spirit world.

Inaabam had also brought his talking stick.

The men looked at each other. Finally, Aajim's father stood to speak. The Shaman passed him the stick.

Aajim had never been close enough to get a good look at a talking stick. This was the first council meeting he had attended. Though sitting outside the circle, he was able to see that Inaabam's stick was about arm's length, carved and decorated with eagle and owl feathers.

Mikinaak slipped the stick into his belt, walked over to the Dakota spear and jerked it from the ground. He hefted it with obvious distaste, looking carefully at its feathers, other decorations and markings. He carried it back to the meeting circle and drove its stone point into the ground.

"The evil one who made this spear is taunting us,"

he said, his rage barely controlled. "He dares us to find him and seek our revenge. And we will. But now is not the time. We must honor and bury our dead. We must work to rebuild our shelters and replace what has been looted. We can't leave our village in this state and unprotected. When we are ready, we will find him and"—he pulled the weapon from the ground and made a quick, symbolic thrust—"run his spear through his black heart!"

He sat down among the murmuring elders. Aajim watched as each considered his father's words. It was obvious all were not in agreement.

One of the men, *Gookooko'oo*, Owl, stood nervously and took the stick. He was not accustomed to speaking out, but his anger gave him courage. His son was one of the two kidnapped children.

"We should let the women care for the dead and follow the raiders while the trail is fresh, while there's still time to catch them. Revenge is the best way both to honor the dead and to regain the honor of our band. There will be plenty of time to mourn after we have returned with many scalps!"

He hesitated and then sat down. His cry for immediate action was met by several war whoops from some council members and other young men and boys sitting with Aajim outside the circle.

The discussion continued with each man speaking in turn. When all had spoken, the medicine man stood and took the stick. As the band's spiritual leader, he spoke with almost as much authority as the absent chief. He was one of the elders who had survived the raid. But his daughter was among the dead.

"I have lost more than many of you." He stopped and looked at each council member, his eyes burning with reflected firelight. "But we cannot abandon our people in this condition—with dead to honor and a village to rebuild. The time for revenge will come. But it is not now."

He remained standing and called for a vote. While not unanimous, the majority favored delaying any attempt to avenge the dead and to make the Dakota pay for their insult. The decision led to an angry outcry, particularly among the young and hot headed. A group, led by *Keeshegkoni*, Burning Fire, stood, and, with obvious disgust, melted into the night.

Because Aajim had friends among the young dissenters, he joined them as they converged on another campfire to vent dissatisfaction with their elders.

Aajim watched as Keeshegkoni threw more wood on the fire and dropped to his haunches, staring intently at the dancing flames. He was well named. Outspoken, self-centered, strong, quick to anger, Keeshegkoni, although he had only 16 falls, was already a force to be reckoned with. Aajim could see he was very angry.

Keeshegkoni had accompanied the men on the hunt and had taken one of the deer—his first kill as part of a formal hunting party. When gutting the deer before their return, he had been given the heart. It was his to roast and eat before the band in celebration of his skill as a hunter. But the Dakota raid had stolen his chance for recognition. With obvious disgust, Keeshegkoni pulled the heart from the hide bag still slung on his shoulder and threw it into the flames. He watched as it blackened and sizzled.

The other boys gathered in small groups. Some talked quietly about the day's events. Others muttered their disappointment with their elders' inaction. Still others watched Keeshegkoni fuming in front of the fire, his face contorted with rage. They were waiting for the inevitable explosion. They didn't have long to wait.

Suddenly Keeshegkoni stood and whirled to face the boys and young men. Silhouetted by the fire, his was an imposing figure—tall for his age and muscular.

"They are a bunch of old women," he said with contempt. "The honor of our band has been despoiled and they do nothing. The enemy is still within our grasp, but they mewl like cougar kittens. They, too, are blind and clawless. We will make the Dakota pay, they say. When? When they find their courage? The time to strike is now.

"Aajim, you gave the warning. How many raiders were there?"

Aajim was surprised by the question. Keeshegkoni almost never addressed him. He hesitated, trying to construct an answer.

"I'm not sure. It all happened so fast. It was foggy. I think I saw maybe eight or 10."

Keeshegkoni considered his answer.

"We would easily outnumber them. They will be easy to follow. They will have to move slowly, burdened as they are with our goods and two captives. We could be on them before they knew it."

He stopped to let his words sink in.

Aajim thought he understood what Keeshegkoni was saying, but he wasn't sure the others did. By "we" he meant those who were listening to his words, not the "old women" against whom he raged.

"Let us organize our own war party. Let us avenge our dead and restore honor to our band. Who's with me?"

His question was answered with stunned silence.

Finally, Aajim's brother spoke.

"You would have us go against the ruling of the council? And, even if we wanted to, how could we organize a war party under their very noses?"

"Everything is so confused I think it would be easy," was his response. "We would each pack our own food. Most of us have weapons. Some could be borrowed from the men. We'd travel fast and light—knives, spears, bows, axes and shields. We would leave before dawn."

More silence.

Miskwaanak, Red Cloud, spoke. He had accompanied the men on the hunt and returned to find his grandmother slain.

"I, too, want revenge so badly I can taste it. But we are not yet warriors. I don't think we have the skill to defeat the raiders. Dying ourselves will not avenge our dead or restore honor to our band."

Keeshegkoni didn't like to be challenged. Aajim thought he seemed to grow even larger as he delivered his response.

"It is the attempt that matters, not what happens. The attempt, not what happens," he repeated.

"We must do this. If not, I will go alone. I will not attend this spring's Gathering with my head hung low. I will not endure the shame. I will not be looked down upon by members of the other bands. And I will not be rejected by a girl because she and her family view our band as weak and unworthy of respect.

"Do what you want. I will be waiting before dawn by bench rock for those brave enough to join me."

Chapter 3

THE DECISION

The boys watched Keeshegkoni stomp from the gathering and fade into the night's gloom. They milled about, furtively glancing at one another, looking for signs of reaction. Most were stone faced; their thoughts unreadable.

Keeshegkoni's challenge was not to be taken lightly. Refusal to take part in the attempt at revenge, no matter how unlikely its success, could be viewed as cowardice. No boy verging on manhood wanted to earn that label, one that he could carry for the rest of his life.

Aajim looked at his brother. Animikil's face, too, was impassive. But Aajim thought he detected anger just beneath the surface of his unreadable expression. Animikil returned his gaze and walked around the fire to join him. Others had begun to form in small groups of close friends. The boys had been raised together; had known one another all their lives. But, of course, cliques had developed over the years. Discussions about the war party, Aajim suspected, would take place within these small groups of trusted friends.

"Damn him!" was the first thing Animikil said on joining his brother. "That hothead has put us all in an impossible position. If we say 'no,' we're cowards; if we say 'yes,' I fear we'll all die. Even if we outnumber them, I doubt we have the skill to defeat seasoned warriors."

Animikil thought. "Of course," he said, "they might be young bucks raiding to make names for themselves. Why else would they have struck so far into our lands this early in the year? Did you see any of them clearly?"

"As I told Keeshegkoni, it all happened too fast. I'm not even sure there weren't more than eight or 10."

Aajim looked at his brother and asked quietly, "What if the elders learned of Keeshegkoni's plan? Wouldn't that be a way to stop it?"

Animikil took him roughly by the shoulders. "Who would tell the council? You? He would certainly find out. Are you prepared to face his wrath? In any case, even if the council tried to stop him, he would still find a way to go—even if by himself. He would become a martyred hero and we'd still be cowards.

"Remember what he said? 'It's the attempt, not what happens.' I think he really believes that!"

"So, what will you do?" Aajim asked.

"I don't know. I must think. Everyone will have to make his own decision."

"Well," Aajim said, "if you go, *I* go."

Animikil again took him by the shoulders. "Look at me and listen, little brother. If I go, you will *not*. If I go, I will probably not return. You will be our parents' only son. You are too young, too inexperienced. If you go, we both may die. And I'm more likely to die if I have to look out for you."

He gave his shoulders one last shake and then he wrapped his arms around him. He spoke softly.

"I may not see you again. Give my love to our parents and sisters and take good care of them."

And he was gone.

––––––––

Aajim was stunned. As he watched Animikil slip into the dark, thoughts streaked randomly through his mind like fireflies in a summer meadow.

How could I *not* go and still be able to hold my head high? But am I too young to be called a coward? He hated to admit it, but that might be so. He had not yet been initiated into the clan as an adult. His vision quest—during which he would fast, pray and dream to seek his life-long spirit helper— was planned for early summer.

To escape joining the war party that way, however, did not provide any real comfort.

He walked back to the fading fire and hunkered down. Keeshegkoni's blackened deer heart was still visible—a lump of charred flesh. The smell of burned meat tainted the air.

I might do well in a fight, Aajim thought as he watched patterns of red heat skitter through the embers. I am almost as big as Animikil. I shoot a bow and throw a spear as accurately as he does, though without quite as much range. What if the raiders *were* youngsters trying to prove themselves as warriors? If that's the case, we might be more evenly matched. Young Anishinaabe often did the same. In fact, he'd heard talk among some of the older boys—led, of course, by Keeshegkoni—about organizing a raid later that spring.

But how could I go? Animikil has rejected me; the others will follow his lead.

Suddenly Aajim felt very tired. The gut-wrenching events of the long day, the arguments, the emotions held in check, were beginning to take their toll. He closed his eyes. The fire's embers continued to burn behind his eyelids. They quickly coalesced into the bloody face of Omiimii, her lustrous black hair ripped from her forehead.

He stood, tears pooling in his eyes. Somehow, I *will* avenge her death! But how? The answer wasn't long in coming. If they won't let me come, Aajim thought, I will follow them. I will stay close enough so, when the battle begins, I, too, can fight for our honor.

———

Food, weapons and clothing. How can I get them without being seen? Aajim walked toward the remains of his family's hut. A small fire flickered outside the wigwam. His father had apparently cut new poles on which to rehang what was left of the hide covering. He stopped and watched. No one appeared to be around. Noise elsewhere in the village indicated there was lots of activity. Perhaps his parents were helping others.

Aajim slipped into the hut. In the gloom he saw his sisters sleeping under fur blankets, their faces peaceful. Everything was still in disarray, but he was able to find his hide pack. In it he kept the obsidian knife flaked for him by his father, a woven rope snare for small animals, his medicine bag and fire-making tools.

There was also room for food. Searching quickly, he found pemmican and pieces of deer meat freshly roasted that night. He also grabbed a few of the mushrooms he'd gathered earlier and some dried berries and nuts. He took only a little, enough for a few days. He didn't want to deplete his family's meagre food supply. If he were gone longer, he'd have to forage for himself.

Theirs was one of the last huts the raiders came to, so they hadn't had time to make off with any weapons. They lay in a heap on the floor. Among them were Aajim's spear, bow and quiver. There were also several stone war clubs and axes. He grabbed his spear, bow, arrows, and one of the smaller axes. He did not yet have his own shield.

He sat and quickly replaced his camp moccasins with heavier calf-high boots. Digging through a pile of clothing, he found his winter shirt and leggings. The nights were still cold. He stuffed them in his pack.

What else he wondered? If I've forgotten anything, I'll just have to make do.

It was then Aajim fully realized what he was doing. The shock hit him like the lightning bolt that exploded a nearby tree last summer, knocking him off his feet and sending a tingling sensation from his head to toe.

This is the first time I'll venture out of the village for any distance on my own. I won't have the company of the others. And there's a good chance I'm not coming back.

To calm himself, Aajim removed his medicine pouch from the pack and held it, closing his eyes.

He was too young for the pouch to contain many objects to comfort him or speak of his spiritual or clan identity. In it was the small, crude clay figure of wolf, his clan's totem; a rare piece of *miskwaabik*, copper, given to him by his father. There was also the foot of the first *waabooz*, rabbit, he had taken with his bow; a robin's feather to remind him of Opiche and his only remembrance of Omiimii—a pebble sparkling with gold flecks she found in the stream their last time together.

He took one final look at his sisters. He reached down and stroked their sleep-tousled hair.

———

Aajim wasn't sure where to go. It was hours before

dawn and the meeting by the lake of those, if any, who would comprise the war party.

Opiche. The medicine bag now hanging under his shirt reminded him of his sister. Her grave was some distance from the village and not near any beaten path. He would wait with her.

The slim sickle of *dibik-giizis*, moon, peeked from behind long, narrow clouds floating across the sky like canoes. It was more than enough light to take him to Opiche. Since his visit that morning, several delicate flowers had bloomed on her tree, ghostly white in the moonlight. Somehow the sight cheered him. New life among the death.

He took his winter shirt from the pack and slipped it over his head. He pulled on the heavy leggings to provide another layer of warmth. He sat against the trunk of a tall red pine that blocked the slight but cold breeze blowing from the northwest.

His mind wandered. He wondered what Animikil had decided. Then he realized he'd seen no sign that his brother had visited the hut to take his weapons or other things he would need. His distinctly decorated hide shield was still there. What if he'd decided *not* to go? What if I'm sitting here ready to go to war *without* my brother? Would he be at bench rock? If not, I will not be a part of this.

At some point he fell asleep.

———

He woke in the half light of early dawn. Am I too

late, he wondered as he quickly gathered his things and headed for the rendezvous? He knew he'd have to avoid the usual trail to the beach. Others would go that way. Instead he climbed a lesser-used trail that led to an overlook.

He lay down, carefully positioning himself at the edge of the steep cliff. The moon was settling in the west, its fading light illuminating the jumbled ice pack driven inshore by waves. A light fog along the beach was slowly lifting. Aajim looked down the rocky beach and picked out bench rock and the gnarled pine just behind it. There he saw a knot of people gathered around the rock. He counted eleven and then a twelfth appeared from down the beach and joined the group.

He scanned the crowd looking for Animikil. The distance and swirling fog made it difficult, but he finally saw him standing with his back to the rest, gazing out over Gichigami.

Aajim would have to wait until they passed before he could begin to shadow them. He stretched out on his stomach and put his head down to rest.

Am I really going to do this? He could feel Omiimii's pebble in the medicine bag pushing against his chest.

Yes.

Chapter 4

WAR PARTY

It wasn't long before Aajim sensed movement on the beach below. He raised his head slightly. The war party was moving quickly past his position, silently, in single file. He confirmed that there were 12. As might be expected, Keeshegkoni led. He appeared to be carrying the spear the raiders left behind to taunt them. *Inaabiwin*, Lightning, the shaman's son, was right behind.

The rest of the party included his brother; *Biimidoon*, Twisted Mouth; *Mangizide*, Big Foot; *Gaagaagiw*, Raven; *Gizhiibatoo*, Runs Fast; *Miscowaagosh*, Red Fox; *Amik*, Beaver; *Oshkagoojin*, New Moon; *Makwa*, Bear; *Mikige,* Finds Things. Several other boys had been wounded in the raid or apparently chosen not to join the mission.

Though the light was dim, he could see that some had managed to apply war paint. Where they got it was a mystery since the paint had to be mixed fresh using berries, leaves, bark or minerals combined with water and grease. There hadn't been time. Some of his friends liked to practice painting themselves before engaging in mock battles and weapons play. Perhaps they had saved some.

Keeshegkoni's paint was most visible. Half his face was bright yellow, his eye on that side surrounded by a black oval. A black line ran from his forehead down his nose to his chin, separating the two sides of his face. Aajim had seen him wear the paint scheme before. Inaabiwin, appropriately, had stylized red lightning bolts on his cheeks that were outlined in black. Amik had two black hands, fingers outstretched, running from each side of his mouth up his red-painted cheeks. Oshkagoojin, his twin, had the opposite—fingers in red on black-painted cheeks. Some of the others had simpler designs; primarily combinations of red, black, yellow or white stripes—the sacred colors.

The pace was fast but measured. The party moved with a minimum of exertion, conserving energy to cover long distance. This is what their fathers had taught them. Aajim had never seen a war party or group of hunters on the move from a high vantage point before. They moved as one, sinuously, like a snake. There was almost no noise; the procession was ghost like. Foot falls were muffled by the soft leather soles of their moccasins. Arrows were carefully packed in their quivers so they wouldn't rattle. There was no talking, none of the joking or good-natured ribbing he'd come to expect from his friends.

Aajim rolled over and watched the last stars wink out as dawn slowly began to claim the sky. He'd have to wait to follow until the group disappeared around a headland about a mile down the beach. He let his mind wander. Idly, he looked down at his feet. They pointed straight skyward, the result of the way they were wrapped in his cradleboard as an infant. The board's foot rest was designed to force a baby's legs and feet to grow straight, eventually making his stride longer to cover more distance with less energy.

Well, Aajim thought, I guess I'll soon find out how well *that* works.

He hadn't eaten much since the day before the attack, so he pulled a piece of pemmican from his pack and began to chew the tough, dried meat, softening it with his saliva.

The cliff was too steep to descend, so he began working his way slowly back down the hill toward the beach trail. Soon the village would awaken. When would the boys be missed? How long would it take the elders to figure out why they were gone? How soon before an angry search party formed to track them down?

Initially, Aajim had wondered why his friends had chosen to travel on the rocky beach. Now he understood. Not only could they move fast; they'd leave virtually no trail for a search party to follow.

He knew they would turn south—inland—at some point to try to pick up the trail of the westward-bound Dakota.

He reached the beach just as the last of the party disappeared behind the headland. He would have to hurry to stay close enough to see their eventual entry point into the forest.

As he walked, he was aware of the continuous slap of waves on the rocky shore. The gradually melting ice sheets undulated with the wave action, creaking and cracking. He gazed over the lake. There was no horizon; gray water and gray sky melted together.

Gichigami. Home of the Anishinaabe almost since before memory. The old stories told of migration from the east, from the Great Salt Water where their ancestors had lived, a migration that had taken many generations. Some medicine men had prophesized that a tribe of white people was coming from across the great ocean and would destroy them. They were told to travel west until they came to a land in which food grew on water.

When they finally came to Gichigami, the migrants split. Some traveled north to look for the land of the prophesy. Others continued to search along the south shore. Many years later, the two groups met after circling the huge lake and found a bay they called Zhaagawaamikaang, a place of shallow waters. It was the land where wild rice grew on water. Initially they settled on the largest of 13 islands in the bay. They called it Mooningwanekaaning, island of the yellow-shafted flicker.

So it was known that Gichigami was huge—a wild and unpredictable force of nature to be revered and reckoned with. Whenever Aajim was near the lake he could feel its restlessness, its power. It was changeless but always changing.

Stories around campfires often included tales about Gichigami. Aajim's favorite was about *Mishibizhii*, Underwater Panther, master of all water creatures. The storyteller often was *Madaagamin*, Turbulent Water. He told of fishing on the lake. He did not realize he had gone far out when a big storm engulfed him. As he paddled madly to regain the shore, he saw Mishibizhii jumping from wave top to wave top in delight, its red eyes burning. It had the head and paws of a giant cat—a lynx or panther—but was covered with scales like a fish, with dagger-like spikes running down its back and tail. Soon the waves were so high and rain so heavy Madaagamin couldn't see the shore. But Mishibizhii jumped ahead and seemed to be inviting him to follow. Once the shore was again in sight, the creature disappeared beneath the waves.

He approached the promontory. He had been here when much younger, fishing with his father and Animikil. Several enormous boulders jutted into the water. One was topped with an ancient, stunted *giizhik*, white cedar, growing from a crack it had created in the massive rock.

Aajim had never seen boulders this large. Nor had he

seen a rock split by the power of a living thing. In wonder he'd asked his father where such massive rocks came from and how a tree could break one asunder. Mikinaak looked down at him, a half smile forming on his lips.

"Perhaps you should have been named 'asker of questions' instead of 'tell a story.'" He had become accustomed to his young son's curiosity.

They walked on for a short time. Aajim waited. He knew his father was forming an answer.

"There is much we know, but more we do not. Why is the sky blue? Why does the wind blow? What makes the waves on the waters of Gichigami? Where do the stars go during the day and why do they sometimes fall? How does the rice grow?

"What we *do not* know we accept as the work of *Gichi-Manidoo*, the Great Spirit, Creator of all things, Giver of Life. The things we *do* know, we have had to learn. We know He gave us *waawaashkeshi*, deer. But we had to learn how to make use of His gift. He gave us *ishkode*, fire. But we had to tame it.

"I, too, have wondered about the power of this old tree," he said. "I think it reminds us that the spirit of living things is strong, stronger even than the stone upon which the world rests.

"That's my explanation," he said. "But it may be a question you would like to ask Inaabam. The medicine man may have another idea."

Aajim was just able to skirt the base of the boulders

and keep his feet dry. Green, orange and black lichen grew in profusion on the gray faces of the towering stones. He stepped slowly around the point and stared down the long expanse of beach. No sign of the war party. The boys must have gone inland somewhere along this stretch.

Now, he thought, I'll need to test my limited tracking skills. He walked to the tree line and, gazing down, moved slowly along the edge of the beach looking for telltale signs of entry. He soon came to a small stream bursting from the woods, frothing with snow melt, making its way across the rocky beach to be welcomed by Gichigami. One of the boys had been careless. A fresh moccasin print appeared in sand at the edge of the stream.

Thirsty, Aajim stooped to scoop water from a quiet pool. As he stood, he saw something reflected in the water; the image wavy in the ripples. He looked up and floating above him on the strong breeze off the lake was Giniw, golden eagle. He was amazed by the size of the bird; by the way it hung motionless without apparent effort. He wondered if Giniw were watching him. An instant later—it seemed longer—the bird gave a full-throated scream, wheeled around and headed inland over the stream.

A sign? He turned and followed the stream—and the eagle—into the forest.

Chapter 5

TRACKING

A narrow path followed the stream inland, a trail cut by forest animals to give them access to the lake. The trail was well worn and muddy with fresh moccasin impressions. Aajim had gone only a short distance before he had also seen deer, elk and moose tracks intermingled with tracks of those who hunt them—wolf, lynx and cougar.

He saw no black bear tracks, but knew makwa were plentiful. They had just come out of hibernation and were hungry. Fortunately, they rarely ate flesh. Still, this time of year, they could be dangerous, especially a female with cubs.

Makwa, probably his best friend, was somewhere ahead. Last fall he had gone on his vision quest and emerged from the sweat lodge to tell the medicine man and his family he'd dreamed makwa was his spirit guide and that he wanted to take the name "Bear." Aajim hadn't thought much about it at the time. Among the men, names often were not permanent. Experiences or revelations from the spirit world later in life could lead them to shed a name like snakeskin and take another.

But, over time, Aajim came to think Makwa was well named. Like makwa, he was a little slow in thought and action. But he was big, strong, resilient and could be stubborn. And, like his namesake, he could, if provoked during games or weapons practice, move with speed and ferocity.

Aajim wasn't surprised Makwa had joined the war party. He doubted his friend had given it too much thought. He would go where his friends went.

As he moved through the silent forest—silent because the war party had driven wildlife deeper into the woods or caused them in hunker down quietly in place—Aajim, for the first time, felt lonely. Giniw had long since disappeared, the direction or purpose of his journey unknowable. Other birds were silent—robin, sparrow, chickadee. There was no rat-a-tat of the red-headed or black-backed woodpeckers.

Not for the first time he wondered how his parents were feeling now they had discovered the disappearance of their two sons. He thought again about Animikil's admonition:

"If I go, I will probably not return. You will be our parents' only son."

Am I being selfish? Why am I going, knowing my death would devastate my family, possibly leaving no male to carry on our bloodline? Is it to avenge

Omiimii? Is it to regain the honor of our band? Is it to prove I am brave, that I deserve respect? Is any of this worth the price I may pay, my family may pay?

Aajim sensed the stream was starting to angle east. As the war party had done, he would soon need to leave the relatively easy travel it afforded and turn into the forest. He squatted and took a long drink. He was getting warm. He splashed the ice-cold water on his face. The water trickled down his neck. It felt good. He stood, removed and packed his heavy shirt. To satisfy hunger pangs, he ate a handful of dried berries and nuts.

It was not difficult to find where the war party had left the trail. Even an inexperienced tracker could find traces of 24 moccasins. He continued south, making his way through dense forest while absently noting trees of special interest to his people—the paper birch, sugar maple, spruce and pine.

The conifers wore their year-around dark green coats. Seed cones from last season littered the ground.

The oaks, as was their habit, had retained many leaves from the previous autumn. They shivered in shades of brown, rattling dryly in the light breeze, and would fall as new leaves grew. The birch and poplar were already showing some new leaves; the maple would follow.

The thick canopy overhead kept much of the sunlight from reaching the forest floor. So, except for ferns, some brush and fallen trees, the hilly ground was quite open. Much of it was covered with a soft blanket of pine needles, making tracking more difficult. Still, he was usually able to keep on course. Several times he went for some distance without seeing signs. So he zigzagged east and then west until he again crossed their path.

He wondered how far ahead the war party was. He knew they'd be traveling fast. Had they found the Dakota's trail yet?

Chapter 6

THE BOYS

The day wore on, still with no sign that the war party had found the Dakota's trail.

To occupy his mind as he walked, Aajim began to think about the boys whose footprints he followed. Some he knew well; some of the others—the older ones in particular—not as well. He wondered what they were thinking as the time for confronting the enemy neared.

There was, of course, the perpetually angry Keeshagkoni—belligerent, mean-spirited, aloof, easily offended, confrontational, physically powerful. In leading the war party, he was in his element. It was said someday he might lead the band. Others wondered if he had the right personality for leadership.

Inaabiwin looked a great deal like his father, Inaabam, the shaman. But that's where the similarity ended. He had chosen a path far different from his father's. He and Keeshagkoni were much alike, both in build and personality. The two were close in age and had been friends since early childhood. But it was said that Inaabiwin was impressionable and had been influenced by his volatile friend and not the other way around. Inaabam, clearly unhappy with what his son was becoming, had not been able to alter his path.

Brother Animikil, almost two years Aajim's elder, was quiet, thoughtful, resourceful and already a skilled hunter. And he had a spiritual side. Though he had fasted and meditated days longer than usual, Animikil emerged from his vision quest without dreaming of a spirit guide, something that rarely happened. At first he thought himself a failure. However, the shaman considered it a sign and had taken an interest in him. They talked a great deal. Inaabam might, in secret, be grooming him for entry into the *Midewiwin*, the Grand Medicine Society, to study and, himself, become a medicine man.

Biimidoon was his cousin. They had played together when young, although a few years separated them. Now he was part of the older group of boys. Biimidoon's father, perhaps the most skilled tracker in the band, had taught him the craft well, so well it is said the son tracks as well as the father. Aajim guessed his friend would be out ahead of the war party, looking for signs of the enemy's trail. And, oddly, his father would undoubtedly lead the party that would search for them.

Mangizide, Big Foot. Rarely ever had a name meant less in describing its holder. Nothing about

Mangizide was big. He was small in stature, older by a year than Aajim, but shorter. After the naming ceremony, his parents assumed the medicine man had dreamed he would grow to some size—big feet, big man. So the naming led some to wonder if the shaman had ingested bad mushrooms that day. Mangizide was waiting for a sign from the spirit world that would suggest a more appropriate name.

Because Mangizide was small, he was quick and agile. And, because he was small, he had learned effective tricks to defend himself in rough and tumble with friends.

Gaagaagiw was the silent one. His mother had died at birth. His father was killed only a few years later in a skirmish with a Dakota hunting party. As is the custom, he went to live in his uncle's household. It was not a happy place. *Bookojaane,* Broken Nose, was not a good provider and there were many children. Gaagaagiw was ignored and grew up lonely and bitter. Though others tried to help him, he didn't know how to accept or give friendship. He spent a great deal of time alone in the forest and learned much about the behavior of its creatures. It was even rumored he could commune with them.

Aajim remembered that the suspicion was reinforced one day when Gaagaagiw and two others were returning from fishing. A large male bear burst from the undergrowth just ahead of them. The boys froze. The bear rose on his hind legs to full height, growled menacingly and pawed the air. In panic, the others turned and fled—exactly the wrong thing to do. Gaagaagiw calmly stood his ground, allowing the boys to escape. Later he explained that running, showing fear, just incites makwa. Standing quietly, making no eye contact, is the best tactic.

If the Shaman had erred in naming Mangizide, he made up for it when he named Gizhiibatoo, Runs Fast. Now 16, he was so fleet of foot he had won every race at last fall's Gathering. Long and lanky, his legs were a blur when he ran full out. It was good he had this commendable skill since he was not physically attractive. Large noses are prized among the Anishinaabe, but, as he grew, Gizhiibatoo developed the largest nose anyone had ever seen. It was the subject of much mirth, particularly among the girls. Because it was sometimes runny, he became known as Nose Runs Fast. If he knew of the unkind nickname, he never let on.

Miscowaagosh, Red Fox, unlike his namesake, was anything but sly or crafty. He was, in fact, rather simple, gullible and often the butt of practical jokes perpetrated by the boys. Aajim remembered one trick. Miscowaagosh's fear of snakes was well known. When he was with a small hunting party, Amik, one of the twins, found a large but harmless bull snake. While Miscowaagosh was in the bushes relieving himself, the boy crammed it in his pack. When he returned and picked it up, the snake stuck its head out, flicking its long tongue. With a shout, he dropped it and ran crashing into the woods. In a minute, he returned, laughing. That's one of the things his friends liked about him. He was good natured. He never seemed to get angry when teased, but laughed along with the teasers.

Amik and Oshkagoojin were the only *niizhoode*, twins, in the band. As it is with twins, the two were inseparable and, when dressed alike, delighted in swapping identities. This was to be expected of twins. It is said that the mythical *Nanabozho*, the trickster, son of the West Wind, had a twin brother. Aajim had been taught that Nanabozho is a virtuous hero, dedicated friend and teacher of humanity. Though he may behave in mischievous, foolish or humorous ways, Nanabozho never commits crimes or disrespects Anishinaabe culture. He is viewed with great respect and affection. It remained to be seen how virtuous the twins—joksters both—would be. It was no surprise the two—mirror images tied as they were by mystical bonds of birth—would both join the war party.

Aajim ran through the list of war party members in his mind. He suspected he had forgotten someone.

Ah, he thought, Mikige. He was new to the group of boys, so it had been easy to overlook him. His family had lived at some distance in a small band whose totem, like that of Aajim's, was Wolf. Ma'iingan was a relatively large clan among the Anishinaabe with numerous related bands.

Mikige's band had fallen on hard times. Its summer camp was located near the ever-changing border with the Dakota and an enemy raid—far more devastating than the one his people had just suffered—wiped out so much of its population that survivors dispersed to join other bands within the clan. The boy, who had lost his father and two siblings in the raid, was withdrawn and had yet to make much of an impression. Aajim suspected he joined the war party for reasons of his own.

He came to a small stream and stopped for a drink. He slipped off his pack and pulled out a piece of deer meat. Chewing as he walked, Aajim thought about Mikige's plight. What, he wondered, would happen if few or none of the war party returned. His band was not large. Would the loss of so many young men and boys—much of a generation—eventually mean its end? So much talent would be lost. The thought frightened him. It made him want to run to catch the group before it encountered the enemy; run to try to change the boys' minds.

Chapter 7

THE FIGHT

Aajim sensed that the weather was changing. The wind had picked up and blew from a new direction. The slate gray cloud cover had lowered and scurried over the forest, hiding the tops of the tallest of the red pine. It was colder and he smelled rain.

He stopped briefly and took his heavy shirt out again. It had a hood.

I'd better move more quickly, he told himself. Aajim knew that rain, particularly if it were heavy, would obliterate the signs he was tracking. At least it wasn't cold enough to snow, although that, too, could change.

He took off at a slow trot. At one point, it appeared the group had picked up and followed a south-ward-heading animal trail, making both tracking and jogging easier.

But, as the first drops began to fall, the animal trail veered west. The boys continued south. In minutes the rain was heavy. He pulled up his hood. At first he could still make out some signs, but they were quickly disappearing in the dark and downpour.

Now what? I can't keep up this pace. I'll have to slow to look more carefully for tracks.

He had gone only a few more feet when there was great confusion in the signs. At last, he thought. The group had found the Dakota trail and followed it west. He did the same.

The rain slackened a bit. The trail, because it was created by two war parties, had become larger and much easier to follow. The rain soon stopped but was replaced by *awan*, fog, that swirled slowly between the rain-darkened tree trunks.

The reality of what he was doing hit him in the gut. How far ahead are the boys and will I get there in time to join the fight? Part of him hoped not! He felt shame.

He ran along the now obvious trail, stopping every minute or two to listen. The fog seemed to muffle forest sounds. Once he thought he heard noise far ahead, but he couldn't be sure. He ran on, heart pounding. He stopped again. This time he was certain he heard faint shouting. Has the fight already begun?

He soon came to the top of a small rise and, as he started to work his way down, saw movement ahead. He circled to the right, staying low to the ground behind ferns and fallen trees to get a better view. He bellied under a fallen tree trunk and, looking at the small valley below, saw something he couldn't understand.

With their spears, Dakota warriors had herded most of the boys into a circle. Most were unarmed and appeared unhurt. He watched as several of the enemy dragged two bodies a short way back down the trail and then strung them up from their wrists to trees on either side. Who were they? He couldn't tell from this distance.

Meanwhile, others began to tie the boys together at the waist. They're captives, Aajim realized. As they tied them, the Dakota joked among themselves, slapped, pushed the boys and threatened them with spears and axes. Soon they gave each one a large bundle to carry—the furs, hides and other items they had stolen from the village. He could see having beasts of burden to carry loads *they* had carried made the Dakota very happy.

Before the party started moving, the two missing children were brought out of the woods and each given to one of the boys to mind.

Aajim watched in disbelief as the enemy and their captives—nine of his friends, his brother, he hoped, and two children—disappeared into the fog.

———————

Aajim backed out from under the trunk and sat for a moment, leaning against its wet, mossy bark. What had happened here? It didn't appear the war party put up much of a fight—two killed and the rest taken captive, unharmed. He had noticed there were more warriors than he had thought when they invaded the village. They were not young Dakota out to make a name for themselves. These were seasoned warriors.

And who had been killed and put on display in such a barbarous manner? Aajim hoped one wasn't Animikil.

He back tracked to the trail and scrambled down into the small valley where the confrontation had taken place. As he walked he came closer and closer to the bodies shrouded in fog, hung unceremoniously from tree limbs overarching the trail. They had not been hung high; their legs were bent at the knee. Their bodies were slouched; heads resting on their chests.

As he approached the first body, he knew instantly who it was. The yellow paint on his face identified him as Keeshagkoni. Blood from his scalping had run in profusion down his face, mixing with the war paint to create an unforgettably grisly picture. His eyes were open. His mouth was twisted in pain, anger and frustration.

He must have put up a real fight. Spear thrusts had pierced his bloody buckskins several times; he had suffered a crushing blow to the side of his head.

A few feet further on hung the body of Inaabi-win, son of the shaman and Keeshagkoni's faithful companion. He had suffered an ax blow to his neck that almost severed his head from his body. His shirt and leggings were soaked in blood.

Aajim bent over and threw up what little he had in his stomach.

Unable to look at the bodies any longer, he walked a short distance down the trail, pulled off his sodden pack and sat on a log among signs of the confrontation. A large splotch of blood was not far from where he sat, probably marking the place where one of the boys fell. He looked more closely and saw parallel lines in the muddy forest floor leading toward the bodies. He wondered who had died on that spot.

He couldn't imagine how they had been caught off guard and surrounded. It finally occurred to him that the Dakota may have staged an ambush. But how could they have known where or when to set it up? Perhaps scouts had been positioned in the rear to watch for the expected revenge-seekers? Once spotted, they could have run ahead and warned the others.

Aajim looked around. The site was perfect for an ambush. The narrow valley served as a funnel. The Dakota would have secreted themselves on the up slopes and swept down upon and surrounded the unsuspecting boys. But why did only Keeshagkoni and Inaabiwin die? Why weren't they all killed?

Against all odds, Keeshagkoni may have resisted, hoping the others would join and fight. But only Inaabiwin followed his lead.

He would probably never know.

———————

Aajim was at a loss as to what to do next. His head was spinning. He was exhausted, cold, hungry. The physical and mental strain of past two days had drained him. He closed his eyes and tried to get mind and body under control. The rain had started again.

I've got to do something. But what? Part of him wanted to cut the boys down. I can't leave them like that, he thought. Another part of him cried to turn around and flee. It was all he could do to stop from grabbing his pack and running back the way he came. Maybe he would meet the search party he imagined was trying to follow them. He could lead them to the Dakota. In the ensuing battle, they might rescue the boys and regain the band's honor.

But how good were the chances he could find them? Or they him? The heavy rains had obliterated tracking signs. Even Biimidoon's father, the best tracker in the band, would find conditions next to impossible.

Or, it occurred to him that he could follow the enemy, learn where they had taken the boys and then return to the village with the location. The thought scared him, but a little voice in his head said this is what he should do.

He stood, slung the pack over his shoulders, pulled the knife from his belt and approached the bodies to cut them down. He had his hand on Inaabiwin's wrist but thought again. As much as he disliked the idea, he wondered if it weren't better to leave them hanging in case the search party came upon the site of the fight. It might give the searchers a better idea of what had happened here. It certainly would provide an incentive for them to continue the search.

So, instead, Aajim reached under the boys' shirts, cut their medicine bags free and placed them in his pack. In case they weren't found, he hoped to be able to return the sacred possessions to their families.

Chapter 8

Giniw

Having made the decision to continue to track the Dakota was one thing. Actually mustering the courage to start down the trail was another.

Night was coming. It came early in the deep forest; even earlier on stormy nights such as this. And it was getting colder. Aajim knew he had to find shelter for the night. But not here. There was always talk of ghosts around the campfires; stories about how spirits of the dead—especially those who died horrible deaths—would remain to haunt the places where they died. The hauntings would continue until their bodies were buried properly with appropriate ceremony. He hoped Keeshagkoni and Innabiwin would eventually be honored and laid to rest.

He walked down the trail, wind-blown rain in his face. It wasn't long before he found what he was looking for. The young burr oak had a split trunk about four feet off the ground. A small stand of spruce was nearby. He used his ax to cut large limbs from the bottoms of several. He dragged them back to the oak and hung the limbs from the notch, resting them on the ground to form a small shelter.

Pushing his pack and weapons ahead of him, Aajim crawled into the tight space. He rearranged the branches to provide as much protection as possible from the rain and wind. He knew his body heat would help warm the small shelter. It was too wet to make a fire.

He pulled a piece of pemmican from the pack. That, a handful of nuts and berries and a couple of mushrooms were all he allowed himself. He kept the remainder of the deer meat in reserve. He knew food was going to be a problem since he hadn't imagined he'd be gone this long.

As he chewed the pemmican, he pushed the pack against the trunk to use as a pillow. He couldn't stretch out for lack of space. So, he lay on his side and curled up. He was not comfortable and wondered if he'd be able to sleep. Fortunately, the forest floor was soft. Consumed by exhaustion, he drifted off.

He was running down a trail. He didn't know if it were to or from something. As he ran, Aajim noticed a strange thing. The faster he ran, the lighter his body seemed. He almost felt as if he could fly. And so he did. He jumped and felt weightlessness. He rose and kept rising, soon above the trees that spread below like a green carpet. The sky above was bright blue and sprinkled with clouds, brilliant in their whiteness. He felt happiness and a freedom he had never known.

How can this be? He stretched out his arms to help maneuver. But they were not his arms. They were wings, the wings of Giniw, golden eagle. He felt their strength as they rhythmically beat the air. He watched as feathers on his wingtips moved to control the direction of flight. Our wingtips, Aajim thought. For we seem to be one. He felt not two but one heart beating strongly as they fought to stay aloft, fought the fact that everything must eventually return to Earth.

The cold wind ruffled their feathers. He realized they were spiraling skyward, looking for updrafts to ease their effort. The motion made him dizzy. The sun, which now seemed ever so much closer, bathed them in golden light.

Soon warm air rising from the ground provided a cushion on which they could soar. They resumed their original direction, southwest Aajim thought, and continued—to what or where he did not know.

Gradually the forest thinned. To their left was a small encampment along a stream. It was Dakota. Aajim knew because of its three cone shaped dwellings—teepees. It was the first time he'd seen them.

Instead of flying on, Giniw/Aajim circled the camp. Except for one cooking fire, it seemed deserted. Odd, thought Aajim. There should be the bustle of early morning activity.

They screamed the eagle's powerful cry. As they did, a figure emerged from one teepee—a young woman, perhaps a girl, with a long black braid. She looked skyward. Aajim was shocked. It could have been Omiimii. She walked with a limp to the fire to stir a pot suspended on a tripod. She looked up again as they banked and resumed their journey.

Below, clearly visible, was a well-worn trail. Ahead, seeing with the eagle's powerful vision, they detected movement. Soon they overflew a long line of marchers. It was the Dakota and their captives. The boys were in the center of the line carrying bundles; their captors in the front and rear.

Giniw/Aajim wheeled and made another pass. They screamed. Several boys looked up. Aajim saw the faces of Animikil and his friend, Makwa. They banked, left the marchers behind, and again followed the trail.

Aajim had never seen the prairie. It stretched to the horizon. There were few trees. Grasses waived in the wind. There were small streams, several crossing the trail. Ponds and lakes dotted the landscape. The sun reflecting in their waters turned them silver or made them sparkle with points of light.

As they flew, Giniw/Aajim felt hunger. It grew stronger. They surveyed the landscape looking for a meal. Soon the eagle's sharp eyes spotted movement. With folded wings, they dove on an unwary hare. Before it could scurry to the safety of its burrow, their talons bit flesh and they flew on, the hare struggling weakly in their grasp. Such was the power of the eagle that they barely felt its weight.

They alighted next to a pond, quickly broke the rabbit's neck and began to tear at the warm flesh. He had never tasted anything better. Once sated, they left the carcass and hopped to the nearby water to drink and wash blood from their beak and feathery face.

As they resumed flight, Aajim felt a sleepy contentment and he noticed a peculiar thing. The sun was moving quickly in the sky. Soon it sank in the west surrounded by a host of red, orange and yellow clouds.

In the light of the setting sun, Aajim saw smoky haze on the horizon. Soon a huge camp came into view. It stretched along the shores of a lake. It looked temporary and he recognized it for what it was—a large Spring Gathering where Dakota clans would, as did his people, meet to trade, socialize, sing, dance and drum, compete in games, and—for the young—look for suitable mates.

So this, Aajim realized, is where his friends were being taken. Their captors were going to show them off at the gathering along with evidence of their raid into Anishinaabe territory. They would, no doubt, bathe in the praise of fellow warriors and enhance their reputations for daring and bravery.

But what then, Aajim wondered, would happen to his brother and friends?

He awoke slowly, aware of something heavy on his chest. A branch had fallen on him, probably resulting from his restless sleep in that small space. Spruce needles covered his face. Their pungent aroma filled his nostrils. At least the rain had stopped sometime overnight.

He pushed the branch off, stood shakily and took the rest of the shelter apart. It was just past dawn. Looking up through the tall pines, he saw clear sky.

Aajim was famished. Hunger gnawed at his stomach. He took a piece of meat from his pack—one of the few remaining—and sat against the trunk of the oak and tore at it with his teeth. It was tough, dry and didn't taste at all like the fresh, raw rabbit he'd consumed as Giniw. Suddenly, remembering the taste of the bloody flesh brought details of the dream flooding back.

If I can believe the dream, he thought, I know where the boys are being taken. It's a large Spring Gathering of the Dakota. How far it was he couldn't tell, although it did appear to be to the southwest. Time seemed to have been compressed during the dream, but the encampment could be less than two days distant.

If true rang in his head. It was, after all, a dream, but a dream unlike any he'd ever had. In many ways it had seemed so real. He remembered the feeling of flight, of Giniw's powerful wings propelling them through the air, of diving on the prey, the taste of raw rabbit flesh. He remembered the small village and girl with the braid, the upturned faces of his brother and best friend, the sun dappled ponds and lakes.

Did I imagine all that? He remembered stories some of his older friends told of dreams during their vision quests. The dreams, they said, were so real, so vivid. But *their* dreams resulted from days of fasting and praying. What led to *my* dream? Perhaps I don't need to go on a vision quest. Perhaps Giniw is my spirit guide and helper. I didn't have to seek him; he seems to have sought me? But that's not the way it's supposed to work.

Again Aajim faced a decision. Can I believe what I have dreamed? Can I return to my people and tell them I dreamed where the boys have been taken? Or should I continue following to try to learn for certain where they are and what is their fate?

Then the realization hit him. Even if his people knew the location, what could be done? The band was too small to attack an entire Gathering to rescue the boys. Other Ma'iingan bands would have to be recruited for any chance of success. It's doubtful that a war party could be raised in time to save the boys from whatever fate is to befall them.

The situation, thought Aajim, is hopeless. I have no reason to believe the dream is true. And, even if it were, there's nothing The People can do about it.

The pull of home was strong, but the unwanted voice in his head again whispered that he should follow. He had to try to learn the fate of his brother and the others.

Chapter 9

THE GIRL WITH THE BRAID

Aajim repacked, tucked the ax in his belt, slung the bow and quiver over his shoulder and took spear in hand. He wondered whether he would ever have need of them.

Once on the trail, he turned his attention to food. He was very hungry, but had only a piece of meat and a couple of mushrooms left. He'd have to forage for food, something not easily done in early spring.

He wished he had paid more attention to his mother's instructions. She was a skilled forager—in any season. Although gathering, like almost everything else, was women's work, she wanted her boys to be able to take care of themselves if circumstances required.

Well, thought Aajim, they do *now*.

As he walked, he tried to remember her instructions. Mushrooms, for certain. But he had to be careful since many were poisonous. The spikey ones he picked earlier were fine, although she had warned there are poisonous ones that look something like them. Another he remembered grew on downed, decaying trees. It was flat, brown and, like its host, a bit woody.

He could look for early berries. There were also edible roots and tubers, but he doubted he could recognize the plants. In any case, he'd have to dig them up. He didn't have time.

For other edible plants, he would probably have to explore streams and ponds. In spring, *apuk'we*, cattail, shoots were edible as was watercress. He also might be able to spear fish. Bird eggs were a possibility if he could find nests he could reach.

Serious hunting was out of the question. He didn't have time to stalk, kill, butcher and roast game. He might get lucky and bring down a squirrel or hare. But, again, there would be no time to cook the meat. While the rabbit he ate raw when Giniw/ Aajim was delicious, that was only a dream. He preferred roasted meat. In any case, building a fire was probably not safe.

Mushrooms and eggs might be easiest, so he left the trail and went deeper into the woods, walking parallel to the path. And if I come to water, he thought, I'll stop and look.

———

He walked for some time before finding mushrooms. He broke them off a dead tree trunk. They *were* woody and without much taste. He saw several nests, but they would have been a difficult climb. It would take more energy to harvest the small eggs—assuming there were any this early—than it was worth.

He noticed that, gradually, the forest was thinning. Sunlight filtered through the canopy and pooled on the forest floor. He returned to the trail.

It was afternoon and Aajim felt the need to hurry to catch up. Then it occurred to him that the Dakota might still have warriors trailing behind to watch for more following Anishinaabe. So I can't get too close because, as forest becomes prairie, I will be even easier to spot.

Soon the landscape consisted primarily of tall, dead grasses. He could see shoots of green; new growth to the replace the old. In many places the grass was taller than he. The trail had become more like a tunnel. Signs of the war party and its captives were easy to spot. They were not far ahead.

He heard running water. A small, swollen stream crossed the path just ahead. To the left he noticed a stand of cattails some distance up river. As he walked along the muddy bank to harvest new shoots to add to his meagre food supply, he caught a faint whiff of smoke. He looked up and, to his amazement, saw the tops of three teepees above the grasses along the bank.

The girl with the braid? Was this the small camp on a stream Giniw/Aajim saw from the air? Could the dream be true? He crouched and waded quietly across the narrow stream. He had to find out.

Aajim slowly pushed his way into the tall grass and began to crawl. The going was difficult, but he had to hide himself from view. Nearing the edge of the camp, he put down his weapons and pack and slithered the last few feet. Still hidden in the grass, he had a good view. It appeared deserted. A single fire smoldered in front of the nearest teepee. A pot hung on a tripod over the fire just as in the dream. But no sign of the girl.

Aajim lay there considering his options. I should get back to the trail. I think I've seen enough, he thought, to prove the dream may have been more than a dream. But as he started backing away on his belly, the teepee flap opened and out stepped the girl with the braid. It was her. She walked, with a slight limp, carrying wood to the fire pit.

She *did* look like Omiimii, who frequently wore her hair braided. But it was more than the long braid falling down her back. Despite the limp, she moved with Omiimii's grace. Even their faces were similar.

Lying on his stomach, as he did earlier watching the ill-fated war party gather, Aajim felt Omiimii's pebble press against his chest. He knew he had to find some way to meet the girl of the dream.

———

He watched her add wood to the fire. She went back to the teepee, returning shortly with ingredients for a meal. They went into the pot. Some sort of stew, Aajim guessed. It wasn't much food, but, obviously, she was cooking for more than one. She sat on a log and idly poked the fire.

There was a barely intelligible screech from inside the teepee. The girl sat for a moment longer, then stood and returned to the dwelling, resignation on her face. Once she was inside, Aajim heard the shrill, cackling voice of what sounded like an old woman. Soon the girl came out carrying a pot. She walked to the stream, emptied it and returned to the teepee.

He again carefully surveyed the rest of the camp. Still no sign of anyone, not even camp dogs. A thought came to him. Is it possible everyone else has gone to the gathering he saw when Giniw/Aajim, leaving the girl behind to care for an old woman?

The sun was now low in the west. He had to decide how to approach the girl before it got too dark.

The stew was bubbling in the caldron. The smell of food almost made him dizzy. When she returned to the fire, Aajim was afraid she would hear the loud rumblings, grumblings of his stomach. She ladled stew into a bowl and returned to the dwelling.

Let her eat and feed the old one first, he thought. Then I'll make my move. But, what move? I can't just stand up and surprise her. She would see I'm not Dakota. Would she run for a weapon—or just run? I can't assure her. I don't know the language.

Then Aajim remembered sign language tribes used to bridge language barriers. He had never signed, but knew a little. Growing up, the boys would sometimes practice with the help of an adult. Does she know any? What can I "say" to keep her from panicking?

Raising the right hand, palm out, was a non-threatening greeting. He was also pretty sure he could manage "don't be afraid." He remembered the sign—actually two signs—for Anishinaabe. "People" and "tree." The sign for Dakota, on the other hand, was "cut off the head" made by drawing the right hand flat across the neck from the left. Maybe if I told her I was just hungry—drawing my little finger across the center of his body as if cutting it in two—she would feel some compassion.

In a few minutes—it seemed much longer—she returned to the fire, ladled some stew into a bowl and sat.

It must be now. Aajim stood and walked slowly into the camp, heart pounding. She looked up; he stopped and raised his right hand in greeting. Her reaction was not at all what he expected. There was initial surprise. She stiffened and looked carefully at him. Then, of all things, she smiled. It was a small smile, but unmistakable. Perhaps, Aajim thought, the girl is simple.

Before he could sign "don't be afraid," she asked, pointing at him, "Anishinaabe?"

Aajim nodded. She then pointed to herself. "Anishinaabe." She smiled a much broader smile. He must have looked confused. She held her arms out, crossing her hands at the wrist. The universal sign for "prisoner." She then showed him six fingers.

Aajim understood. He nodded and smiled back. She was a slave captured at age six. And she apparently had retained some of the language.

He pointed to himself. "Aajim." She repeated his name. Pointing to herself. "*Uvver-gah Hoo*."

Realizing he couldn't speak Dakota, she tried to translate the name into Anishinaabe but didn't have the words. She clenched both fists, put them together and then twisted them violently down at the wrists. "Broken." Then she pointed to her leg.

She is called "Broken Leg," Aajim translated.

He asked her Anishinaabe name. "*Minochige*," she said. He translated, "Do Things Well."

"I will call you Minochige," he said.

Minochige fed him well that night. Once she made certain the old woman was sleeping, she brought out more ingredients for the stew and two sleeping robes to wrap around their shoulders as the evening cooled.

They were shy with each other. Conversation was difficult, but got easier as more of the language returned to her.

She thought she was 13 and didn't remember exactly how she came to be captured. She believed the people of her band were attacked as they moved from spring to summer camp and didn't know if her parents and brother were dead or alive.

She said, eyes downcast, her captor was "*inigaa*," mean to her. As she got older, he made her do much of the work that his two wives had done. When about 10, she ran off, only to be quickly recaptured.

"Broke leg so not run," she said in a small voice. "'Grandmother,'" she nodded to the teepee, "fix."

Seeing the distress on his face, she said, "No hurt."

That smile again.

She told him—mainly by signing—that earlier in the day she had seen young Anishinaabe captives being herded on the trail heading for the gathering.

"You follow?"

Aajim tried to explain the thwarted effort to avenge the attack on his village and that he had to learn the fate of his brother and friends. His people had to know.

Minochige shook her head. "I want help, but...." She looked at the teepee. "She good to me."

There was an awkward silence. He looked at her beautiful fire-lit face, and, without thinking, said, "I will come back for you."

She looked up at him. He saw hope but also doubt. He was ashamed he had made such a promise—a promise he probably could not keep.

As his father had said: "Promises are like spider webs—easily blown away by the winds of fate."

———

Aajim slept by the side of the teepee, covered with a buffalo robe blanket. Minochige made him as comfortable as possible. She knelt beside him.

"I must go before sunrise," he said.

"I wake you," she promised. She paused. It was as if she wanted to say more. Instead, she stood. Silhouetted by the fading firelight, and walked to the door of the tent.

Why, he wondered, would Giniw have shown

him these things? Why would he have led him to Minochige? He wished he could ask the shaman for an explanation. He again regretted promising to rescue her from the abuse she was forced to endure. But he wanted to take her back to her people.

He could leave with her *before* her captors returned. But that would mean abandoning his mission; it would also mean she would have to abandon her "grandmother," something she wouldn't do. Minochige was well named—"do things well." Despite the cost, she honored her commitments.

No, he vowed, I will go to the gathering and learn what I can. Then I will come back and try to take her from this place.

Sleep would not come. He gazed skyward. The stars were bright. *Waabigoni-giizis,* Flowering Moon, had not yet risen. He realized he was able to see the night sky almost from horizon to horizon, something impossible to do in the forests of the Anishinaabe.

He tried to relax by searching for familiar star formations he had learned as a child—Biboon-Kenoni, Winter Maker, with his arms, legs and belt. And there was the curly tail of Mishibizhii, the great underwater panther. Almost directly overhead was *Ojiig-anang,* Fisher. The dipper-like group of stars is said to bring summer as it moves across the sky. When overhead, the Fisher signals that tapping for the maples can begin.

———————

Minochige woke him by gently shaking his shoulder. It

took him a while to remember where he was and why.

"Come," she said. "Almost dawn."

Aajim stood stiffly and shook the heavy dew off the blanket. She had brought the fire back to life and heated last night's stew. As he sat, she put a bowl in his hands, went into the teepee and quickly returned with food and clothing.

"Pemmican and fish," she said.

"*Miigwech*," thanks.

She handed him some clothes.

"Wear these. Look Dakota."

The heavy deerskin shirt did differ in design and decoration from his own. The leggings had fringe down the sides. He tried on moccasins she provided. They were different in construction and too big.

As a finishing touch, she gathered his long hair from behind and pulled it through a carved bone ring. She then inserted three golden eagle feathers. Giniw, thought Aajim. It somehow seemed right.

She stood back and smiled. "Better," she said.

For a moment they faced each other in the awkward silence of goodbye.

Finally, "Be careful." She quickly kissed him on the cheek, turned and retreated to the teepee.

Aajim watched her go and stood for a moment wondering what it was he was feeling. The last thing he wanted to do at that moment was leave. But there was no other way.

Chapter 10

THE GATHERING

He knew he had to stay off the main trail. Minochige had warned him it was heavily traveled. The gathering was about a day's walk.

The going wasn't easy. He was usually swimming through a sea of tall grass. Once in a while he happened upon an animal trail heading in nearly the right direction. As he had seen as Giniw/Aajim, there was much water. He frequently had to walk around ponds, small lakes or wade streams. There was some open prairie without much cover. He missed the deep forest where he could simply melt into the trees and undergrowth.

He drank at streams or ponds when thirsty, but ate while walking to cover as much ground as possible. Even so, he feared he would not reach his destination before sundown.

And what will I do when I get there? He imagined a gathering of this size would be very busy, bustling with activity. If it were anything like Anishinaabe gatherings, there would be drumming, dancing and singing, contests of skill and competitions of all sorts. People would be preoccupied with socializing and trading goods. If I were simply to walk into the village, I might not even be noticed.

As sunset neared, the sky suddenly filled with early flights of noisy *nikag*, geese, heading north to their summer nesting places. Later in spring, the skies would literally darken as the large gray birds passed overhead in numbers too large to count. In the woods of the Anishinaabe, their passing was much less dramatic. But, here on the prairie, one would be able to see the many layers of arrow-head-like flights and hear their incessant calls.

Aajim once asked his father why the geese flew in such precise formations. Mikinaak confessed not to know but suggested, perhaps as a joke, that the arrow shape pointed in the right direction and helped them find their way.

Soon he smelled smoke on the wind. It had to be the gathering. The land fell away and, in the distance, he saw dozens of cooking fires twinkling in the twilight. There hundreds of teepees gathered around the large lake Giniw/Aajim had seen before he awoke from the "dream."

He lay in grass on the bluff above the village. It was still some distance and he believed he'd be safe there overnight. But he wondered if it would be less dangerous to enter the camp under the cover of darkness? There would only be firelight. And nights usually were boisterous with music, bonfires, storytelling and feasting. It's possible no one would pay much attention to him.

On the other hand, although the cloak of darkness might keep him safe, it also might not allow him to learn anything about the boys. And so it was that he decided to spend the night on the lonely, windswept bluff.

Aajim stayed low and cut tall tufts of grass to serve as bedding and to cover himself during the long, cold night. The grass might not warm him, but it would help keep him from being soaked with dew.

He chewed some pemmican and watched the village fade into darkness. Soon several bonfires blossomed. And, as expected, the night air was punctuated with the incessant sound of drums pounding out ancient rhythms of the Dakota. Voices of singers rose and fell from high-pitched screams to deep rumblings as they told tales known only to listeners and dancers gathered around the fiercely burning fire.

He wondered if Animikil and the boys were still alive and hearing the same music.

I still don't understand why they all weren't killed on the spot. Surely the Dakota kept them alive for more than simply to serve as bearers for stolen goods. He reconsidered his original idea. They must have been brought to the gathering as proof of their captors' prowess, bravery. And, once the boys had been paraded and shown off, once the braves had received the acclaim and accolades they sought? Then what? The boys were too old to be made slaves. With a sinking feeling, Aajim knew their sentence was death.

Despite a knot in his stomach and the boisterous sounds from the camp, Aajim eventually fell into a deep and dreamless sleep.

The sun, peeking unimpaired over the flat eastern horizon, brought him back to life. He let consciousness slowly wash over him. The knot in his stomach was gone, but, as soon as he began to think about what the day might bring, it again tightened into a fist.

He threw off the wet grasses, crawled some distance away from the lip of the bluff and relieved himself. Breakfast, for a welcomed change, was dried fish. He wondered if Minochige had caught the fish in the stream running through camp; if she had cleaned and smoked them.

He looked down at the village. Little stirred. Its inhabitants were apparently still asleep, recovering from the night's festivities.

I should probably go now before the camp comes back to life.

He hid his pack and weapons, except for his knife, under the grass he'd used for bedding. Weapons were not allowed at Anishinaabe gatherings. He imagined Dakota would have similar restrictions. In any case, walking into camp with a pack and weapons could only draw attention.

Now, he wondered, should I simply enter the village from my position on the bluff? Or should I work my way over and use the trail. He didn't like the open country between him and the camp. He could be spotted long before he reached it. He decided to use the trail, assuming it would be without much traffic this early.

Before leaving this last place of hiding, Aajim decided it was a time for prayer; time to open his heart to Gichi-Manidoo, the great Creator, and seek His help. He first envisioned Giniw, for it was the eagle who was said to carry prayers to God. His prayer was simple: "Help me this day to find my friends, learn of their fate and return safely to my people." He thought to include rescuing Minochige in his prayer, but didn't want to ask for more than he thought he deserved.

The trail was a short distance to his left. Soon he was hidden in grass on the hillside above it. It was empty as far as he could see in either direction. He worked his way diagonally down the slope and headed quickly for the gathering.

He had walked only a short way before two figures materialized from a copse of small trees on the other side of road. A young man and a girl about his age. They were obviously surprised to see him and quickly walked ahead toward the village. As they walked, the girl ran her fingers through waist-length raven hair to remove kinks. The boy adjusted his leggings.

Sex was not a mystery to Aajim. He was aware

of his parent's lovemaking in the small confines of their hut. And, of course, the young men of the band liked to boast of their conquests—real or imagined. Gatherings were a hotbed of sexual excitement as young people from different bands sought mates.

Soon the trail hooked to the right and into the camp. Teepees of various sizes lined up two or three deep on both sides of the wide pathway. To the left was the lake, bordered with reeds and cattails. Pulled up on shore were several canoes. Unlike Anishinaabe boats made with birch bark stretched over wooden frames, Dakota canoes used deer hide.

Women had started building cooking fires. Children were filtering out of dwellings to warm themselves by the fires and wait for the morning meal. No one seemed to notice Aajim as he walked by as casually as he could. Even the camp dogs appeared more interested in waiting for breakfast scraps than investigating the stranger passing by.

Somewhere along the way, the two lovers separated, returning to their families to answer good-natured questions about where and with whom they had spent the night.

Aajim began to feel more comfortable. This is going much easier than I expected, he thought.

Ahead, at the end of the path, was a large circular area. In its center smoldered one of last night's bonfires. Bordering the open circle, a large teepee caught his attention. Two guards were posted just outside the tent flap. They had spears; axes were in their belts. To the side of the structure was a pile of weapons. Aajim's suspicions were confirmed when he saw his brother's distinctively decorated hide shield in the pile. They were still alive—prisoners.

He showed as little interest as possible and slowly walked by. The guards were bored and didn't even look his way. One stood; the other was on his haunches half asleep. Rather than turn around and draw attention to himself, Aajim walked toward the lake to get away from the village. He had to decide what to do now he had found the boys alive.

Deep in thought, he walked along the shore unaware of quiet footsteps behind him. He was surprised to hear: "Hey, my young friend, are you lost?"

Aajim reacted quickly, turned, and said: "No, I'm just looking...." Then he realized the question had been asked in Anishinaabe and that he had answered in Anishinaabe. The big smile on the face of his questioner told the story. He had been tricked.

He immediately turned and ran. Behind him he heard the young brave repeatedly shouting what he assumed to be "Anishinaabe" in Dakota.

Aajim was fast. Not as fast as Gizhiibatoo, but fast enough. He had a head start, but nowhere to go. Fortunately, the village was still sleepy. Not many people were available to join in the chase.

Then he remembered the canoes. They were only a short way up the shore. To get across the lake was his only chance of escape—a slim one at best. Fortunately, he was good with a canoe. For many falls he had paddled the canoe as his mother pulled wild rice plants over the side and beat rice grains into the bottom of the boat.

There were three canoes, paddles lying on their bottoms. Aajim quickly collected paddles from two and threw them into the center boat. His pursuer, still by himself, was getting close and still yelling. He pushed it into the water and waded out as fast and as far as he could before carefully climbing in. He paddled hard for the middle of the lake. The hide-bound canoe was heavier, slower and rode deeper in the water than canoes with which he was familiar.

Two others had now joined the chase and the three had come to the paddle-less canoes. By then he was a good distance from shore, but still could hear their continued shouts for reinforcements. Aajim paddled furiously and didn't look back. He hoped other paddles weren't readily available.

Then he noticed something. There was water in the bottom of the canoe and its level seemed to be rising. No! The boat was leaking—badly. The water was already over the top of his moccasins and he had nothing with which to bail. It was getting harder to keep the increasingly water-laden craft moving. How long do I have before it sinks?

Alternatives flitted through his mind. There weren't many. The eastern shore was near, but he couldn't swim in the heavy deerskin he was wearing. In any case, the water was almost freezing. He wouldn't get very far.

He turned and paddled toward that near shore. If I get close enough, maybe I can wade. I think the lake is shallow. It would take time for my pursuers to run around to this side of lake. But the boat was half full of water and he could barely make headway.

He heard shouting and turned to look. Two canoes were bearing down on him, each with two paddlers. He'd never make it to shore before being overtaken. The canoe was half full. He plunged a paddle into the water to search for bottom. It struck mud. I could try to wade, but there's not enough time.

The unwelcomed realization came. I'm going to be captured and share the fate of the others.

Chapter II

CAPTIVITY

The two canoes straddled his. In the rear of one was the Anishinaabe speaker.

"Nice try," he smirked. "But looks like you picked the wrong canoe."

The others laughed.

"Now be a good little Anishinaabe and crawl into my boat. If you cause trouble, we'll put a rope on you, throw you in and drag you back to shore."

Aajim complied, his clothing soaked from the waist down. The canoe was small. He sat hunched in the center, shivering.

The other captor in the boat reached over and pulled the eagle feathers from his hair. He said something in Dakota.

"You won't need these anymore," was the translation.

A crowd had gathered on the shore. As the canoes pulled in, the onlookers parted making a path for the little procession. Aajim was in the center being pushed along occasionally by the man behind him.

The crowd was hostile but virtually silent. In it he saw one familiar face. The girl he'd seen returning from the early morning encounter with her boyfriend.

The crowd followed as they walked to the teepee containing the other captives.

How am I going to explain this to Animikil was his only thought?

After a short conference with the guards, the flap was opened and Aajim was unceremoniously and roughly shoved inside. He tripped and went sprawling in a sodden heap on the dirt floor. By the time he sat up, the flap had been closed and the interior was in almost total darkness. Only a shaft of light from the smoke hole falling near the center of the room provided any illumination.

The boys, accustomed as they were to the dim interior, could see better than he. From across the room he heard: "Aajim, that can't be you!" It was Animikil. Soon he was by his side.

"What in the name of the Creator are you doing here?" It was said with both surprise and anger; more statement than question. It hung in the air while he struggled to form an answer. Meanwhile, the others gathered around.

"I followed you. I wanted to help," was his simple response.

Angrily, "Fool! I told you not to come. Now you will die with the rest of us."

————————

The boys were quiet, dispirited, withdrawn.

"What do they plan to do with you...us? Do you know?

Animikil answered. "We don't know, but what are the choices? Enslave us? We're too old. Hold us for hostage? What do our people have they want? They took much of it. We have served the raiding party's purpose—to gain prestige. Now they will kill us. We just don't know how or when."

A long silence followed.

Aajim asked. "What happened on the trail?"

His friend Makwa answered.

"Keeshagkoni led us into an ambush. They must have had a rearguard watching for followers. Before we could react, they surrounded us at spear point and laughed when they saw who we were. One who spoke a little Anishinaabe asked if this were the best our band could do—send children to do men's work. This enraged Keeshagkoni and he, followed as always by Innabiwin, fought and tried to rally us. They were quickly subdued, slaughtered and hung along the trail."

"Yes," Aajim said. "I saw."

"And still you came? You are either very brave or very stupid," Animikil said. "What did you hope to accomplish by following us farther?"

"I wanted to find out where you were taken and your fate. I thought our people should know."

Silence. Before anyone could speak, the flap flew open and water skins and food were dumped on the floor. The flap closed.

The boys converged on the food and drink.

Aajim was confused. "If they are going to kill us, why are we being fed?" he asked, almost to himself.

"This is the first food we've had," Amik said. "They don't want us to die from hunger before they are ready to kill us." It was the kind of darkly humorous observation the boys had come to expect from the twins.

More silence as the boys chewed the very stale pemmican.

Tentatively, Aajim asked, "What about escape?"

An angry voice came from somewhere in the gloom. "Who do you think you are, pup? You just got here. We are guarded. We have no weapons. Do you think they'd just let us walk away?"

"All true." It was Makwa. "But I'd rather die on my feet fighting than be roasted, skinned alive or used for target practice."

There were a couple of grunts of agreement.

"I know I just got here, but I did have a chance to wander in the village. This teepee is at the west end of camp, close to open country. It's not heavily guarded. The two I saw were bored and not really paying attention. Your weapons are in a pile by the side of the tent. If we waited until after tonight's festivities, we could overpower them, climb the bluff just to the north and quickly be among the tall grass. The going is not easy. I came that way. But there would be some light from Flowering Moon. We'd split up and go separately. That would give them 11 different trails to track...."

He stopped, surprised by his outburst.

"Well, what do we have here?" It was one of the twins. "A little war chief in the making?"

Makwa spoke up. "Who has a better plan?"

Before anyone could speak, the flap again flew open and five or six Dakota crowded into the tent brandishing spears and shouting. The boys were herded into the blinding sun of midday. Pushed into single file, they were marched toward the center of the large circle. There, sitting on a stump and surrounded by several warriors, was an old man dressed in unadorned buckskin.

The boys were prodded into a semi-circle around him and forced to kneel. A crowd had gathered.

Standing by his side was the Anishinaabe speaker who led his capture.

He spoke: "This is *Tatankaskah*, White Buffalo, chief the many bands gathered here. It is he who will decide your fate."

"White," thought Aajim. He knew a white buffalo was rare and probably held sacred by the Dakota just as a white deer was revered by the Anishinaabe.

The Chief looked up slowly and surveyed the captives. He *was* old. His mahogany face was creased and lined. It looked like tree bark. A deep scar ran from his forehead cleaving his right eyebrow and then down his cheek. But it was his eye that sent chills down Aajim's spine. It was milky white, dead. The slashing wound had blinded him. It was a nightmare face.

The old chief looked carefully at each boy. Aajim

vowed not to show fear. When the chief's piercing one-eyed gaze reached his face, he made eye contact and returned the stare. Aajim wasn't sure, but he thought he saw a faint smile crack Buffalo's narrow lips.

When through studying the captives, he spoke briefly with a quiet, raspy voice.

"Who will speak for you?" was the translation.

The boys shifted uncomfortably on their knees. Most looked at Animikil.

"I will," was his reluctant reply.

While not the eldest among them, Animikil had often been cast in the role of leader.

Buffalo looked at him. "Why do you bring war to the Dakota?

"They"—looking at some of the war party in the crowd— "attacked our village. Our fathers were hunting. They killed 14 old men, women, mothers and children. They tried to burn the village and stole our goods. We sought to avenge this cowardly attack."

Aajim couldn't believe Animikil had the courage to speak in this way.

The chief considered the translation, face impassive.

"But you are mere boys." He waved his hand in a dismissive gesture. "Why do *you* seek revenge? Where are your fathers?"

Animikil hesitated. It was clear he didn't want to speak ill of their elders. But he had to say something.

"Our village was ruined. Many were killed or injured. The Council voted to set things right before forming a war party."

"So you violated your elders' ruling and came to make your own war on the Dakota?"

"Yes."

The chief shook his head. "I don't understand. Did you really think you could inflict enough injury on your attackers to avenge this insult to your band?"

Again, Animikil hesitated.

"Maybe not," he said. "But in the case of honor, it is the attempt that matters, not what happens." Clearly Animikil remembered, if not the exact words, the essence of what Keeshagkoni had said.

The chief slowly nodded as if in agreement. Again, Aajim thought he detected a slight smile.

Then silence. It seemed as if the old man had gone into a trance. His head fell to his chest, gnarled hands clasped in his lap. No one seemed concerned. The only sound for a short time was the wind blowing across the open circle, forming little dust tornados that whirled, danced and disappeared.

Then the chief raised his head.

"I have listened to what you have said and considered what to do with you. It is not an easy decision. There are those who advise me to have you tortured and killed. It is good advice. We could easily eliminate almost an entire generation of future warriors from your band."

He paused and looked up and down the row of boys.

"But that is not my decision. Your brave and unselfish quest to regain the honor of your band has greatly impressed me. It should serve as a lesson to my own people. You deserve better than death without honor.

"So I offer each of you the chance to fight to the death with one of our young men of the same age. Those of you who survive combat will be allowed to return to your band. Those who do not survive will not be scalped and will be buried with proper ceremony."

He stopped to let his words sink in.

"You will now go and think about what I have said. Those who do not accept my challenge will be put to a quick death."

Chapter 12

THE RULES

The boys were led back to the teepee. Once inside the darkness of the tent, no one spoke right away. Each tried to understand what he'd just heard.

"I've never killed in combat. I've never killed *anyone*. None of us has. We've played at it, but I'm not ready for this." It sounded like the voice of Gizhiibatoo.

"We have three choices." In was Animikil. "Some of us could refuse and be killed. Some could accept combat and possibly be killed. Or we still could try to escape. If we do, some might make it. Those who are caught would certainly be killed."

Silence.

"I will fight. I am here not just to regain the honor of this band. I am here to avenge the death of my father and brothers, the death of *my* band," said Mikige. "We have been offered the chance to live or die with honor. To try to escape would not be honorable."

From Mikige, whom many still considered an

outsider, these words were powerful.

"I don't know if I trust Buffalo," Amik said. "All this talk about honor and respecting our bravery. What if he's just using us to put on a show for the assembled bands? It *is* a gathering, after all. Do we really believe he would sacrifice some of his boys to help us—the enemy—regain the honor of our band? I think he will see to it that we are greatly outmatched and slaughtered."

His statement hung in the air like the slowly floating dust motes.

Further discussion halted when three Dakota entered the tent.

"I am *Akandoo*. At least I was when I was Anishinaabe." It was the brave who led his capture and who translated for the chief. "I was a captive, but chose to become Dakota.

"White Buffalo and I have spoken about his challenge and I'm here to explain how it will work. Combat will be day after tomorrow. Tomorrow you will be given your weapons and allowed to practice—under guard, of course. The order of combat will be oldest to youngest. The chief hopes younger fighters will learn by watching older. As said, each of you will fight someone approximately your own age. Once we know your ages, we will start looking for your opponents.

"Now you need to determine who, if any, among you will not fight. Then you will tell us the ages of your combatants.

"Weapons? You will be limited to spears, axes,

shields and knives. As visitors, you will be allowed to start with weapons of your choice. Your opponents will select weapons to defend themselves. Once combat has begun, weapons may be changed by either combatant at any time.

"Questions?"

"Will there be food?" There was some quiet laughter. It was Makwa for whom having enough food was always a concern.

"Of course. You will be fed as well as any of us. We will not let it be said that we sent you into battle hungry.

"I will return soon to see if anyone declines the challenge and to learn your ages."

The 11 boys gathered around the dim circle of light provided by the smoke hole.

"Amik, do you have more to say about White Buffalo?" Animikil asked.

"No. His actual intentions really don't matter since we have no choice."

"Then let's finish discussing our options. First, is there anyone who will not fight and suffer the consequences?"

Silence.

"What about an attempt to escape?"

Silence.

"Then it's agreed. All will fight. Now let's figure out the order."

Because exact ages to the day weren't known, Animikil suggested they break into groups by year of birth. Then each group would determine oldest and youngest by comparing by the months they were born.

Miscowaagosh, Gaagaagiw and Mikige were 17 and they moved away from the others. The twins, Animikil, and Gizhiibatoo were 16. The 15-year-olds were Makwa, Biimidoon and Mangizide. Aajim was the youngest at 14.

"I guess we know who'll be fighting last," quipped Mangizide.

Once sorted out, the order for the 17-year-olds would be Miscowaagosh, Mikige and Gaagaagiw. They'd be followed by Animikil, the twins and Gizhiibatoo. For the 15-year-olds, the order was Biimidoon, Mangizide and Makwa.

"Maybe the Dakota could find some twins to fight us," suggested Oshkagoojin. It might have been a joke. With those two, thought Aajim, one rarely knew.

"Oh, no!" countered Amik. "I want to go it alone. Otherwise I'll have to fight twice as hard to save us both! We'll draw straws to see who goes first."

There was some laughter. Aajim sensed that the boys were coming to grips with their fate.

But what about me, he wondered? The thought of fighting and maybe dying further tightened the knot in his stomach. His head felt as if it were being squeezed by big hands; a storm of small bright lights flashed behind his eyes.

Chapter 13

PRACTICE

The guards came at dawn. The boys were herded down to the lake so they could relieve themselves and wash up. Food was waiting back at the teepee.

After the meal they were allowed to sort through the pile of weapons, each to retrieve his own. Aajim was empty handed. One of the guards returned his knife, confiscated when he was captured, and then went off to round up weapons for him to use.

The boys were taken under heavy guard to a portion of the large common area to practice. The previous night's bonfire still smoldered.

"You will be allowed to practice all day. Food and drink will be provided." Akandoo had accompanied them.

Biimidoon looked at the others. "I don't think this is a good idea. We shouldn't practice in such an open place. There may be too many eyes upon us, including our opponents. We don't want them knowing how we fight."

Akandoo overheard.

"You make a good point. There is a place near the bluff where no one goes. We will take you there and I'll instruct the guards to keep people away."

Once they completed the short walk, Akandoo smiled crookedly. "Be careful and don't hurt each other." He spoke to the guards and walked away.

The boys milled around, uncertain what to do. Practice? Practice what? And how?

Aajim could sense that Animikil had a plan but was reluctant to put himself forward. However, it didn't take long until the others, as they had done before, looked to him for guidance.

At his suggestion, they sat in a circle, their weapons arrayed in front of them.

"We have played at combat together for years. And our fathers and others have given us various types of training—some more than others. It is unfortunate that ours is a relatively peaceful band. That puts us at a disadvantage against the Dakota who are aggressive and bloodthirsty. It is likely that our opponents will be better fighters than we are; that only the most skilled adversaries will be selected."

He stopped to see if there were any reactions or contributions.

"Do you think we can still try to escape?" It was Amik. Some laughed nervously.

Animikil ignored what he assumed was a joke.

"I think we should review and share what we know before we actually pick up weapons. Since we're limited to spear, ax, shield and knife—and can choose the initial weapon—let's consider what might be a good first choice. Any suggestions?"

"I like the spear," was Oshkagoojin's contribution. "It can keep the enemy at bay to give us a chance to feel him out. The ax requires immediate close-quarters fighting. Then, too, the spear can be used in different ways depending on the opportunities presented."

"And what are those?" Animikil pressed.

Oshkagoojin stood to demonstrate.

"We're more used to throwing the spear when hunting. In hand-to-hand combat, however, it's used primarily for thrusting with a two-hand grip. But there's no reason, if the opportunity arises, not to shift to overhand and throw the spear. The risk is that it takes time to shift grips and back up. If it's not done well and quickly, an opponent can drive his spear home before you can throw. Also, if the spear misses, you'd be weaponless until you can get to your ax."

"We can't forget that the spear can be used for slashing as well as thrusting." Makwa stood, spear in hand.

"To slash, rotate the shaft so the blade is flat. My father says it's good to go for the legs. Opponents are more likely to be defending against body thrusts. If you can cut muscles in the upper leg, your opponent may go down.

"I've also been told that, should he thrust low, it might be possible to knock his spear to the ground and stomp on it, breaking either the shaft or separating it from the blade.

"Gizhiibatoo bring your spear so I can try to break it."

The two faced off and began thrusting, dodging and parrying.

Finally, Makwa parried a low thrust and drove the Gizhiibatoo's spear to the ground. He tried to stomp on the shaft behind the blade. He missed and his opponent quickly had his spear at Makwa's throat.

"Well, it could work—if you're *debizi*, lucky."

"Or if you weren't so clumsy." Oshkagoojin's gibe was met with some laughter.

"We can't assume the opponent will chose initially to defend against the spear with a spear," Animikil warned. "He may choose ax and shield. That would seem to put him at a disadvantage. But a shield can defend against the spear. If he's fast, he may be able to knock the spear away with his shield and rush inside with the ax. So we also need to be ready to use the spear against the ax and shield."

"The ax worries me the most," said Biimidoon. "We don't use axes for hunting, so I've had very little experience with one, except for chopping wood."

Animikil asked if anyone had had combat training with the ax.

"My uncle told me a few things," Mangizide replied. "He said the ax and shield should be carefully coordinated. It's a sort of dance. The enemy swings and you block. Then you swing and he blocks. It can go on like this for some time until one gets tired or careless and the opponent is able to slip a blow inside the other's defenses. It is also possible to fake a low blow, but go high if the enemy is fooled and lowers his shield.

Mangizide picked up his ax and shield and motioned to Biimidoon to join him in front of the group to demonstrate. The two circled each other and, in slow motion, began the deadly dance his uncle had described. Stone ax thudded against shield; ax against shield.

"You dance like two maidens," shouted Gaagaagiw to the amusement of many. Aajim couldn't believe the boys were joking. The good-natured ribbing was probably a way to try to cover their fear.

The two sped up the mock combat. Suddenly Mangizide faked a low blow and Biimidoon, fooled, lowered his shield enough for his opponent to deliver what could have been a fatal blow to his head.

"My opponent tries that and I'll be ready," Biimidoon said. The two sat, panting from the exertion.

Though the air was cool, the sun was hot. Most of the boys removed their hide shirts.

"I know we've practiced throwing axes. But if your opponent has his shield that would be risky," Mangizide continued.

"Then there's the shield itself. If there is an especially hard blow, the ax may penetrate the hide and get stuck. If that happens, it's possible to use your shield to pull the opponent off balance and strike either high or low while his ax is stuck. It may even be possible to pull the ax out of his hand, leaving him defenseless.

"The shield can also be used as a weapon, not just for defense. Especially if you have some size or weight advantage, you could rush the enemy with your shield, push and try to trip him. If he's on the ground, you will have an advantage."

"And what *about* wrestling moves? Like tripping?" Animikil asked.

"Of course, these will not be wrestling matches. But we shouldn't forget that tripping could be useful. You also might have a chance to take him down by dropping to the ground and using a leg sweep," Biimidoon said.

"Does anyone know the leg sweep?" Animikil asked.

Mikige and Gaagaagiw looked at each other; then stood. Mikige had his spear. The two faced off and circled. Mikige shot forward to thrust, but Gaagaagiw dropped below the spear on his haunches and, with one leg, swept Mikige's feet and brought him down.

"I'd like to see someone try that with me," huffed the massive Makwa.

"And knives?" Animikil asked.

"Knives would be a last resort," Gizhiibatoo suggested. "One could only be useful if, for some reason, you have no other weapon—if your spear is broken or if you miss a throw and can't get to your ax. Or somehow you lose your ax—stuck in his shield, for example. Knives work best against knives, not against weapons with longer reach."

"Yes, but don't forget that knives can be thrown," Aajim reminded the group. All the boys had practiced throwing their knives, sometimes in friendly competition.

Animikil looked thoughtful. "I assume our weapons will be placed between us and our opponents when combat starts. So it would be a good idea to try to drive your opponent away, putting yourself between him and his other weapons. That way, should you disarm him or break his spear, he'd only have his knife.

"I also remember my father's advice. Do not let the opponent's movements fool you and do not concentrate on his weapon. Look into his eyes. There you will see his intentions."

Animikil asked if there were any other suggestions.

"If not, let's pair up. We are 11, so there will be one group of three. I will work with my brother."

———

The sun was nearing the horizon when the guards escorted them back to the tent. They were tired, sweaty, dusty and hungry. Though the day had been cool and windy, the boys had worked up a sweat as they practiced the arts of combat as if their lives depended on it. And they did.

Not much was said. There were a few words of encouragement, but, in some ways, the practice session had made several boys even less confident than they had been.

"I felt very awkward as I tried to master all the moves." It was Oshkagoojin. "It's one thing to play at fighting, but something else when it's for real."

Their captors had made an effort to provide a decent meal—fresh fish and venison. But, except for Makwa, few of the boys were very hungry. Bear made sure food didn't go to waste.

They were allowed a small fire, and all gathered around as the cold seeped through the hide walls. Revelry that night was somewhat muted as many of the Dakota had begun preparing to break camp and return to their home villages. The gathering was coming to an end.

But Aajim knew all would stay to see the morning's combat.

———

Animikil and Aajim settled on their backs on the dirt floor and tried to get comfortable. It would be a long night. Wood for the fire was gone and it was reduced to embers that sent sparks spiraling upward to escape through the smoke hole.

Aajim watched their swirling assent, wishing that he could float away with them.

Animikil was silent and then rolled over. Quietly. "You shouldn't be here little brother. This is all my fault."

Aajim was about to ask how that could be. But his brother quickly continued.

"You were right. I should have gone to the elders. We all know that Keeshagkoni was crazy. We let ourselves get sucked into his personal dreams of glory. Now here we are. He was first to die and we're left alone in this nightmare. He knew how to manipulate us. Come with me or be cowards. Come with me and restore the honor of our band.

"I knew better. I think many of us did. But it didn't matter. We didn't want to be called cowards. But we are. We should have been brave enough to say 'no.' Instead, we ignored the wisdom of our elders and willingly lined up to follow that *giiwa-naadizi,* crazy one."

"Then you don't believe we are doing the honorable thing by attempting to avenge the deaths of family and friends." Aajim once again saw Omiimii's blood-streaked face.

"How can killing or being killed by Dakota boys restore our honor? In any case, this was not ours to do. The honorable thing for us would have been to live to become men, to live to marry and raise families, to live to work for the betterment of our band.

"If you survive and I do not, it will be up to you to take care of our parents and sisters. It will be up to you to carry forward our family's legacy. If this is what Gichi-Manidoo intends, I will die more easily because I know I can trust you to take my place."

Animikil rolled over. No more was said. But his words sent chills down Aajim's spine. He doesn't believe any of us will survive tomorrow.

Chapter 14

COMBAT

Despite his exhaustion, sleep was a long time coming. Flowering Moon had risen and Aajim watched as it cast a slowly moving circle of light through the smoke hole onto the floor. As he watched, he was reminded of the night spent next to Minochige's teepee under the vast prairie sky.

Would her captors be in the crowd of spectators tomorrow? Would they return to their encampment and tell her of the bloody combat between the Dakota and Anishinaabe boys? Would she learn of his death or that he lived?

And, if I live, how will I rescue her? First things first, thought Aajim. First, I must survive.

Shortly after dawn, Dakota entered the tent carrying food, water, material to make breechclouts and pots of war paint. They left the flap open to provide more light.

Amik looked at the pile of deerskin pieces. "I hope it's warmer today than yesterday."

They dipped bowls into a large pot of warm stew, drank the broth and chewed the deer meat and pieces of roots and tubers.

The paint provided was yellow, white, black and red—the sacred colors of the Anishinaabe. Aajim assumed they were also sacred to the Dakota.

The boys sorted through the deerskin, each looking for a piece he could use for his breechclout. Reluctantly, they stripped in the still cold teepee. To make a breechclout, a single piece of hide is placed between the legs and then fastened with a belt at the waist. Remaining material hangs over the front and rear giving it a skirt-like appearance.

Makwa had a difficult time finding a piece large enough to cover his substantial girth. The longest piece the tall Gizhiibatoo could find barely provided enough material for front and rear flaps.

Paint provided was enough only for faces. The boys knew war paint, properly applied, was supposed to strike fear in the hearts of the enemy. But no one seemed to believe fiercely painted faces were going to make much difference in the outcomes of their respective fights. Still, knowing it was expected, they paired up and put on the greasy, evil-smelling paint.

Aajim had no idea what design to have Animikil apply. He settled for a white face with black circles around his eyes and horizontal black stripes. He wished he could see the results, but his brother assured him that he would scare his opponent to death. They smiled at his attempted humor.

White Buffalo, accompanied by Akandoo, entered the tent. For once, the former Anishinaabe looked serious.

Buffalo spoke. "We have tried to pick opponents who are as near as possible to your ages," Akandoo translated. "No matter what the outcome, my people are impressed with your bravery and efforts to regain the honor of your band. This day will be talked about among the Dakota for years to come. I hope many of you will be victorious and return to your people so the story also will be known to the Anishinaabe. Be assured that those of you who fall will be treated with proper ceremony and respect. Those who are wounded will be given the best care we can provide."

He paused and looked briefly at each boy. "May *Wakan Tanka* and your Gichi-Manidoo be with you on this day." With a slight bow, he turned and walked into the early morning sunshine.

"It's time," said Akandoo.

A crowd was already formed in a large circle around what would be the field of battle. The boys filed out and, at Akandoo's urging, sorted themselves by age. Miscowaagosh, Red Fox, led the procession. Why, he had wondered earlier, did he have to be first. One of the twins suggested it was because he was the scariest of the lot of them. Slightly simple Miscowaagosh joined in the nervous laughter.

Aajim brought up the rear.

Their opponents were already arrayed in front of the crowd on the other side of the circle. The chief, now wearing an eagle feather war bonnet and his ceremonial robes, walked to the center.

As he began to address the crowd, a large shadow flew across the ground. From above came the powerful scream of Giniw. Aajim was one of many who looked skyward at the majestic bird as it circled the field. Giniw, he thought, please take my prayer to Gichi-Manidoo. Help us acquit ourselves honorably and allow as many of us as possible to return to our families.

The chief finished his short speech, translated by Akandoo for the Anishinaabe, and signaled for the first two combatants to take the field.

It had begun.

———————

Clearly Miscowaagosh was frightened. He looked down the row of his friends for encouragement. Mikige leaned over and spoke quietly to him. Slowly he stood. As always, he didn't want to disappoint. He looked down the row again with a small, wistful smile. Aajim sensed resignation. It was as if the boy knew he would never again see his friends in this life.

His opponent waited impatiently. Miscowaagosh approached, put down his ax and shield and confronted him with his spear. He didn't remember a great deal from the practice session, but he did remember the recommendation that everyone start with the spear.

But the Dakota boy answered his spear with ax and shield. Aajim saw the bewilderment on his face. Oh, no, thought Aajim, Miscowaagosh doesn't know what to do.

The two boys circled tentatively. He thrust several times, but his opponent easily deflected his efforts. Then the Anishinaabe made a deadly mistake. He thrust too hard and too deeply allowing the Dakota to rush him with his shield, knocking the spear aside. He now had nothing with which to defend himself against the coming ax blow. He dropped the spear and raised an arm to block the ax. It bit deeply into his forearm. As the boy pulled the ax free, Miscowaagosh turned to run to try to reach his other weapons. He didn't make it.

The boy cocked his arm and threw the ax at his retreating back. The ax didn't rotate sufficiently to strike blade first. Instead its flat side struck the back of his head with a crushing blow. He crumpled to his knees, then quickly fell face forward and lay perfectly still.

The young Dakota didn't know what to do. Was his opponent dead? It was to be a fight to the death. Someone, possibly his father, shouted from the sidelines. The boy pulled the knife from his belt and approached the motionless Anishinaabe. With more encouragement from the crowd, he knelt and rolled him over. He must have seen death in his face. He stood, tucked the knife into his belt and walked slowly as if in a daze off the field of battle.

Four of the Anishinaabe went to Miscowaagosh's inert body, picked him up by the shoulders and feet and carried him to the shady side of the teepee.

The day had not started well.

———

Mikige, probably because he was new to the band, tried not to show fear. Once Miscowaagosh had been removed from the scene of battle, he stood, bowed his head and, lips moving slightly, said a prayer. He then reached inside his medicine bag, took out three small objects and held them skyward.

Aajim knew Mikige was on a mission that was bigger than avenging the raid on his newly adopted band. He wanted to avenge the deaths of his father and two brothers at the hands of the Dakota; he wanted to avenge the death of his own band. He carried a big burden into battle.

His opponent was slightly larger, but not significantly so. He watched as Mikige picked up his shield and ax. Perhaps, after watching the first contest, he didn't think initiating combat with a spear was a good idea. Instead he drove the spear into the ground and turned to face his opponent who had also chosen the ax.

Mikige wasted no time. With a shout that reverberated around the battlefield, he charged even before the Dakota was ready. Shields clashed and the boy was driven backward, almost tripping over his own feet. Mikige began raining ferocious blows on the boy's shield, driving him to his knees. But, despite the fury of his attack, the enemy kept his composure. Mikige's legs were exposed and, from his kneeling position, the boy lashed out and drove his ax into his left calf.

The blow knocked him off his feet. He tried to stand but couldn't. He could only get up on one knee. Now it was the Dakota's turn to batter his shield with heavy blows. Mikige, too, tried a low blow under the boy's shield, but lost his balance and only succeeded in giving him an opening. With a sickening thud, the ax split his skull.

The Dakota boy, instead of celebrating, looked with shock at his fallen opponent. He reached down to remove his ax, but couldn't make himself do it. Instead he turned aside, bent over and retched.

Members of his family came on the field to escort him off. A man whom Aajim assumed was his father lagged and removed the ax.

The boys carried his body from the field. Animikil walked behind holding his ruined head.

Gaagaagiw had helped carry Mikige to the teepee where he was laid beside Miscowaagosh. They were covered with woven straw mats.

Now it was his turn to fight.

He picked up his weapons and followed blood

trails to the center of the field. The Dakota had not yet arrived. Aajim saw a small knot of people—probably family—surrounding the boy providing encouragement. Sadly, thought Aajim, we have no family to counsel or encourage us.

Gaagaagiw selected his spear; the other boy did the same. They circled each other warily, exchanging several tentative thrusts. Suddenly the Anishinaabe went low with a slashing move. The boy was quick. He jumped back, avoiding the stone blade. But he was now off balance. So Gaagaagiw tried again. This time the enemy was ready. He parried, drove the spear to the ground and stomped on the shaft just behind the blade. The shaft split; the blade dangled.

The Dakota immediately thrust at his opponent's midsection. But he was able to parry and then delivered a blow to the side of his head with the broken shaft. The boy staggered. Gaagaagiw drew his knife and rushed to get inside his defenses. But the enemy thrust his spear between his legs, tripping him. He fell face down. Before he could recover, the Dakota pinned him on his stomach. He grabbed his long hair, pulled his head back and slashed his exposed neck with his knife.

Gaagaagiw struggled, pushing to get up. But the boy kept him pinned as blood pumped from the severed artery in his neck. Only after his body went limp did the boy stand shakily and look at his fallen foe. Blood ran down the side of his face. The blow the Anishinaabe delivered had split his scalp.

———————

Once Gaagaagiw's lifeless form had been carried from the increasingly blood-soaked field, Animikil stood and picked up his weapons. Aajim looked down the row of waiting combatants. He saw shock, disbelief, fear. The three oldest boys were dead in a matter of a few minutes.

Animikil looked at his brother and tried to appear confident. Aajim held his eyes for an instant. They had been close, but there was still much Aajim wanted to say to him, learn from him. He hoped he'd have the chance.

Animikil marched with purpose to meet his opponent at the center of the field. They seemed closely matched physically. He put his ax and shield down and stood, spear in hand. The other boy did the same. Even from a distance his spear looked familiar to Aajim. Animikil recognized it at once. Unmistakably, it was the *taunting* spear.

He looked past the boy at the crowd. Standing in front, a few paces out from the rest, was the leader of the raiding party. He wore a wicked smile. The son would battle the Anishinaabe with the father's spear.

The look on Animikil's face was one of anger, resolve.

The two quickly clashed. The boys skillfully parried each other's thrusts. The battle dragged on for some time in the increasingly warm morning sun. Thrust and parry, thrust and parry. Neither boy seemed to have an advantage.

Then Animikil did something completely unexpected that caused the crowd to gasp. He stepped back several paces, straighten up and dropped the spear to his side, its butt on the ground. He stood motionless and seemed to dare his opponent to charge. The message was the same as that of the taunting spear. "Come and get me if you can."

His opponent couldn't resist. He charged the seemingly defenseless Animikil who continued to stand stock still.

What happened next unfolded so quickly that watchers had a difficult time comprehending it. At just the right instant, Animikil dropped his weapon and deftly side-stepped the taunting spear and its thruster. With both hands he grabbed the spear and wrenched it from his unsuspecting foe's grip as his momentum carried him past.

It took a second for the boy to realize he'd been disarmed. Once he did he sprinted for his ax and shield with Animikil in hot pursuit. The boy dived for his ax and rolled over. From a sitting position he threw it at his oncoming foe just as Animikil threw the taunting spear with all his might. Spear and ax flew past one another, each striking its intended victim.

The taunting spear caught the boy in the middle of his chest with such force that it knocked him flat on his back. He lay there, writhing in pain, the spear standing skyward, its eagle feathers fluttering in the breeze.

But Animikil had not fared much better. The ax

was embedded in his shoulder close to the left side of his neck. Blood pumped from the wound. He fell to his knees and pulled out the ax, causing the wound to bleed even more heavily. Aajim was at his side as he collapsed on his back.

There was wailing from the crowd. In an instant, a shadow fell across Aajim as he cradled his brother's head in his lap. It was the boy's father. It was fortunate there were others with him. Once he determined his son was dead he appeared ready to attack Aajim and his dying brother. He was restrained.

Animikil was still conscious.

"I'm sorry. You *have* to survive," were his last words.

Aajim watched the light fade from his eyes.

The remaining boys were stunned, numb.

Aajim heard Biimidoon say: "He was the best of us. They are too skilled, too fast. They know tricks we do not."

"We have killed one of them," Gizhiibatoo said. "They can be beaten."

Yes, thought Aajim, but Animikil—the best of us—did not survive.

It was Oshkagoojin's turn next. He sat with his twin. They looked at each other. Aajim sensed that some sort of understanding passed between them. The twins stood and faced their remaining friends.

"We were born together. We have always been together," said Oshkagoojin.

"And we will fight and live or die together." Amik finished the statement.

They picked up their weapons and walked toward the battleground. Oshkagoojin's opponent was waiting. The Dakota was confused by what he saw. He looked askance at White Buffalo who was conferring with Akandoo.

The translator met the boys before they reached the center of the field. Aajim couldn't hear the discussion, but it didn't seem heated. In a moment, he returned to Buffalo who listened to the boys' request. He nodded and signaled Amik's opponent also to take the field.

Akandoo addressed the crowd and then translated for the Anishinaabe:

"The twins will be allowed to fight together as a team. The Dakota will fight as a team. It is still a fight to the death."

Amik picked up his spear; Oshkagoojin did the same. Their opponents looked at each other and also picked up spears. From that distance, Aajim and the others could distinguish between the twins only by their paint.

They must have had a plan. The two immediately rushed one of their opponents. Amik thrust high; Oshkagoojin low. The boy, caught by surprise, was only able to parry the thrust at his chest. Oshkagoojin's spear sliced him just above his belt, opening a long and jagged wound along his side. Meanwhile Amik spun around to confront the other boy who was charging to his teammate's aid.

As the two thrust and parried, Oshkagoojin tried to press his advantage. But the boy, despite his wound, defended himself well.

Soon the twins were back-to-back, fighting off their opponents' concerted attack. The wounded boy was losing blood and began to tire. Oshkagoojin picked up the pace, driving the boy back. Amik remained in a parrying duel with his opponent.

Then the wounded boy lunged at Oshkagoojin causing him to lose his balance. The boy threw his spear. It whistled past his ear. Now defenseless, he ran for his ax and shield. Oshkagoojin recovered, ran after him and threw his spear at the boy's back. He, too, missed and had no choice but also to run for his other weapons.

Amik sensed his brother was in trouble, but couldn't disengage. At one point his opponent took a step back and appeared ready to throw his spear. But Amik quickly closed the gap and thrust, requiring the boy to parry. Their dance continued.

Meanwhile, Oshkagoojin's opponent scooped up his ax and shield on the run, turned, and seeing him still rushing for his weapons, threw the ax at his back. This time his aim was true. Aajim saw the weapon strike Oshkagoojin with a sickening crunch in the back just below his neck. He stopped in his tracks, tottered and fell forward on his face like a tree downed in the forest.

The Dakota ran for his spear, intending to help his teammate. But help wasn't needed. Though Amik could not have seen his twin's death, clearly, he felt it. He lost concentration long enough for the boy to step back and throw his spear deep into his chest.

As he lay on his back, clutching the spear with both hands, his adversary knelt by his side, spoke softly and, when it was over, closed his now dead eyes.

———

Aajim didn't think he could watch anymore. Six dead and five left to fight for their lives, himself included. His mind began to drift, attempting to escape the horrors he had seen and the fear of his impending battle. He was Aajim/Giniw again, flying over the prairie, free of all earthly constraints and cares. He saw Omiimii's face, or was it Minochige? He was sitting on bench rock with his father, silently watching the sun rise over the placid early morning face of Gichigami; he and Animikil wrestled in the woods.

Some part of him was aware that Gizhiibatoo had taken the field. At some level, he wondered why the tall, lanky Gizhiibatoo chose the ax and shield when his reach greatly exceeded his opponent's. The fight itself was a blank. Later he vaguely remembered him being carried limply from the field.

———

Biimidoon was next. He seemed frozen in place. Makwa had to help him to his feet. Aajim, through his own fog of fear, could see the resignation on his face; the trancelike way he walked to face his opponent. Aajim bowed his head and closed his eyes. He heard the battering of axes on shields and then tuned even that out.

But these are my friends, he thought. I should honor them by watching. And maybe I will learn something to help me when my turn comes. By the time he opened his eyes and focused on the fight, Biimidoon, bleeding from a head wound, was on his knees defending as best he could against blows raining on his shield. He tried to stand, but his opponent charged with his shield, pushed him to the ground and swiftly finished him with another blow to the head.

The crowd, which had been increasingly quiet, watched in silence as Biimidoon was carried to the sidelines and lined up with the other dead Anishinaabe.

———

Scrappy little Mangizide was next. He tried to cover his fear with a forced smile flashed at his remaining two friends as he picked up his weapons. His opponent, who was substantially taller, smirked and said something in Dakota that was probably derogatory. Despite his opponent's much longer reach, Mangizide selected his spear; his opponent did the same.

The two crouched and began circling. After the Dakota's first thrust, the small Anishinaabe quickly dropped to his knees, scooped up and threw a handful of sand in his opponent's face. The boy was blinded, but reacted quickly. He kept both hands on the spear and slashed wildly in what had been his opponent's direction to try to keep him at bay.

Mangizide quickly circled to the right and moved in to thrust at the boy's unprotected side. But his adversary must have heard or sensed his intentions. He turned in his direction, still slashing from side to side.

Luck was not with Mangizide. As he jabbed, the Dakota's flailing spear sliced his throat, sending him to his knees. Mangizide's forward motion, however, had driven his spear into his opponent's side. The wounded boy, having felt his spear make contact, rubbed the sand out of his eyes. He watched as his opponent frantically tried to stop the river of blood cascading from his neck.

Mangizide slowly sank to a sitting position; his head fell to his chest and he was still.

———————

Makwa sat impassively throughout the slaughter of his friends, showing little emotion. He and Aajim were all that were left. They looked down the empty row where the others had waited their turns for death and realized that it was now Makwa's turn to fight and live or die.

He stood. Aajim stood as well. The two friends looked at each other. Makwa put his hand on Aajim's shoulder. There was nothing to be said. He picked up his weapons and lumbered toward the center of the arena where his opponent already waited.

Makwa kept his spear. The other boy picked up his. The Anishinaabe was about a half a head taller than his opponent; the boy slender by comparison. But, thought Aajim, he looked fast and not at all concerned about his opponent's greater size.

The two crouched in fighting stances. But then something completely unexpected happened. The boy turned away and seemed to run from the field of battle. A surprised Makwa stood, not knowing what to do. The boy, however, didn't run far. Instead, after about 10 paces, he whirled, shifted grips as he turned, and unleashed a powerful throw at Makwa who still stood in confusion. With a bone-crunching sound, the spear point buried itself in his chest up to the shaft.

The boy raised his arms in victory. But Makwa didn't fall. Instead he looked down stupidly at the spear in his chest. He seemed to wonder how it got there. Then he gripped the spear with both hands and, roaring with pain, anger and frustration, pulled it from his chest.

Now it was his opponent's turn to be confused. Makwa rushed him with incredible speed. The boy turned and ran, but he slashed his legs from behind and brought him down. He tried to crawl toward his ax, but Makwa was on him in an instant. He rolled over, held his hands held up in supplication. But Makwa drove the boy's own spear into his chest with such force that it pinned him to the ground.

From the crowd came the keening wail of the dead boy's mother. Makwa fell to his knees and used his hands to try to staunch the rhythmic pumping of blood from his chest. He quickly toppled on his side.

By the time Aajim reached him, he was dead.

Aajim sat in the dust next to his fallen friend. Makwa's and his brother's blood coated his hands, arms and chest. I am the last, he thought. Everyone is dead. I must win. Not only must I avenge the dead of our band—the death of Omiimii—but I must avenge the deaths of my friends.

Enraged, he stood and walked trancelike toward his weapons. Before he reached them, White Buffalo and Akandoo moved to block his path.

Buffalo put a hand on his shoulder: "I am sorry about your friends. All fought bravely and are a credit to your band, to the Anishinaabe. But it's over. There will be no more fighting this day. Someone must return to your people. It must be you. You might not survive your contest. If not, there would be no one left to tell this story."

Aajim wasn't sure he'd heard Akandoo's translation correctly.

"What? Not fight?"

Akandoo nodded.

"Not fight? I must fight! I'd rather be killed than return to my people without avenging our dead. I must fight."

In a rage he tried to push past the two to gather up his weapons. He almost knocked the old chief off his feet.

Akandoo punched him in the stomach, knocking the wind out of him. He crumpled to his knees.

"I'm sorry," he said. "But you must get control of yourself. The chief has decreed that you will not fight. So you will not fight. It is best. The only way your people will learn of their sons' valor is for you to tell them.

"Think! It would probably be easier for you to die here today than to carry this story to your people; for you to be the keeper of this story for the rest of your life. But this is to be your fate."

Aajim remembered his brother's dying words. "You have to survive."

"Come," he said, offering a hand. "We must prepare to honor and bury your friends."

Chapter 15

BURIALS

Aajim sat by his friends and watched old Dakota women prepare them for burial. They washed their bodies and cleaned their wounds as best they could. They had obviously had lots of practice. But, while they were quick and efficient, they were also tender. It didn't seem to matter to them that these were Anishinaabe.

Earlier he had helped them sort through the boys' clothes so they could be properly dressed. Dakota dead, like Anishinaabe, are buried in their best clothing. These, of course, were the only clothes the boys had. But he saw the women brush them to remove dirt and dust accumulated on the trail.

At his request, they had taken spirit bags from around the boys' necks. They sat in a pile in front of him. He would return them to their parents along with those of Keeshagkoni and Inaabiwin.

The women were beginning to sew the boys into deerskin coverings.

A fire had been lit, but there would be no celebration this night. The Dakota were preparing to leave. The gathering was over.

Akandoo appeared out of the gloom and sat next to Aajim.

"They will not be buried in the Anishinaabe way," he said. "The Dakota practice air burial. Hide-covered bodies are placed on wooden scaffolds usually made of lodge poles. Special possessions are placed with the body. The scaffold prevents animals from reaching the body, and allows it to decay naturally."

He explained that scaffolds would be built in the morning.

They sat in silence.

"Are you hungry? Can you sleep?" Akandoo asked.

More silence.

"Why couldn't he just have let us go?"

Akandoo looked for a time at the fire.

"That would not have been possible. Even if he wanted to, that would have made Buffalo seem weak, something no chief can let happen. You have no idea how angry he was with *Chatan*, Hawk, leader of the raiding party, for bringing this problem to him. Chatan should have killed your friends on the spot. Instead he brought them to the gathering to show off. Buffalo didn't say this, but I think he felt the death of his son at the hands your brother was fair punishment for Chatan.

"So, since you came on this quest to restore honor to your band, Buffalo decided to give you the chance to try. All but you have died, yes. But, as your brother said, where honor is concerned, it's the attempt that matters. Now, come. You must sleep. It will be a long day tomorrow and soon you must start your journey."

"I'm not going without my brother. I must take him home. Can you help me?"

Akandoo was silent. The fire burned in his dark eyes.

"I think what you ask is possible. But to drag your brother home will be an ordeal that will test your strength and endurance. If it's what you really want, I will ask Buffalo for permission in the morning."

Aajim looked at the former Anishinaabe and nodded.

A buffalo robe had been spread on the teepee floor; food and water provided. There was a small fire. Aajim was almost reluctant to wash the blood from his body—the blood of his brother and best friend. He dressed in the clothes Minochige had given him. He was surprised to find that the three eagle feathers taken from him on his capture were on top of the pile of clothing.

At first he thought he couldn't sleep, but, as he watched orange sparks float lazily to the smoke hole, he fell into a deep, dreamless state.

The next thing he knew, Akandoo was shaking his shoulder to wake him. It was already mid-morning. He had let him sleep. Just outside the tent, he pointed to a hide-wrapped body strapped with thongs to a wooden frame. Tied to the conveyance was the taunting spear.

"Buffalo thought Animikil should take the spear with him to The Home After Death.

———————

They walked to a hilltop near the encampment. There poles were being strapped together with hide strips. The scaffolds were simple affairs with platforms about six feet off the ground. The hill had been used for burials before—probably many times over many years. Some rickety scaffolds were still standing. The ground was littered with old poles, some of which were being reused.

There were several stunted, leafless trees on the windswept hill. Instead of leaves, they were covered with ravens. The large black birds sat quietly and seemed to watch construction of the scaffolds with interest.

"They always seem to know," said Akandoo. "The Dakota, like the Anishinaabe, believe the raven represents change or transformation. They frequently attend our burials."

Gaagaagiw, Raven, would be honored, thought Aajim. But he wondered if they were really there just waiting for a chance to pick at the corpses.

Aajim counted 12 scaffolds as they neared completion. He realized the two Dakota boys would enter the spirit world with their Anishinaabe opponents.

A procession from the encampment carrying the dead was starting up the hill. Progress was slow. It was led by White Buffalo and a shaman. Among the bearers were the young Dakota combatants. From a distance, Aajim could see them struggling with weight of Makwa. He could also make out Gizhii-batoo's long body and the smaller hide-wrapped package that could only have been Mangizide.

Families and friends followed the two slain Dakota; the men stoic, many of the women wailing in grief.

As the procession snaked slowly past, a girl stepped out of the crowd and walked toward them. It was the girl Aajim had encountered when entering the camp. Walking behind her was the young man. Aajim wasn't certain, but he may have been one of the combatants.

She approached and said something to Akandoo.

"She wants to tell you that she's sorry about your friends and brother."

She continued.

"I am sorry you must mourn alone." She looked away, uncertain what to say next. "I wish you good luck on the journey back to your people."

She returned to her friend who was clearly unhappy that she had spoken to Aajim. He watched them join mourners at a scaffold while the body of a Dakota boy, presumably friend or family, was lifted high and placed upon the platform.

———————

Aajim stood, rooted. Part of him was aware of the ceremony going on around him: the unintelligible sing-song of the shaman as he moved among the dead; the cries of the grief-stricken mothers, grandmothers and sisters of the slain Dakota boys; Buffalo standing stone faced, wind ruffling his feathered bonnet; the ravens still perched in the scrawny trees, ever watchful.

But much of him was elsewhere hiding in some dark place in his mind, unable or unwilling to accept the reality of the nightmare he was experiencing.

———————

Akandoo stayed by his side until the end of the ceremony. Sensing he wanted to be alone with his friends, the translator joined the tail end of the retreating procession.

Aajim wandered among the scaffolds, stopping at each boy to say goodbye. He tried to think good thoughts about his friends, to remember happy times. After spending time with each, Aajim prayed that Gichi-Manidoo would accept his friends and speed them to The Home After Death.

The sun was setting when he finally felt comfortable leaving. It burned the sky crimson, silhouetting the ever-present ravens.

Anger suddenly welled up. He wanted to yell; to kill something. Instead he picked up a rock and hurled it at the ravens. With indignant squawks they took to the sky, their coal-black wings creating a breeze that sent eddies of dust blowing at Aajim.

He turned his back on the burial ground and walked back to the encampment.

Chapter 16

THE JOURNEY

It had been a cold, stormy night. Aajim's fitful sleep was interrupted several times by wind-blown freezing rain and sleet drumming on the hide-covered teepee. To keep warm, he rolled up in the buffalo robe.

When he opened the tent flap, a thin sheet of ice disintegrated, shards clattering on the ground.

Aajim asked to return to the low plateau above camp where he had hidden his pack and weapons. The rising sun was slowly melting ice covering the tall grass. The water droplets sparkled.

It took him a while to find the spot where he'd nested prior to entering camp. He retrieved his things and returned to find Akandoo waiting for him.

"Not the best day, perhaps, to start for home. But the sun should warm your journey."

He pointed to a quantity of food and invited him to fill his pack.

When he was through: "Come, White Buffalo would like to wish you well."

The walk to the chief's teepee was a short one. Clearly preparations were also underway for his departure. On their arrival, an old woman entered the tent. Soon Buffalo joined them. He walked stiffly, his worn body obviously affected by the damp cold.

"So," he said through Akandoo, "you and the others came to seek revenge and restore honor to your band." He stopped and stared intently at Aajim with his one good eye. "Did you accomplish what you came to do? Was"—he waved an arm at the field of battle— "was it worth it?"

Aajim thought but didn't have an answer. "I don't know. So many have died. Maybe when I'm older I will understand these things."

Buffalo's lips cracked with his small smile. "I tell you my young friend," he rasped, "if you come to understand this, and I am still walking the face of the Earth, I hope you will come to me and explain. I have lived long. But I confess that honor is still a mystery to me. Honor is something we seek, yes? But at what price?"

With that he reached into a pouch and pulled out a piece of leather suspended on a thong. On it, drawn in white, was the outline of a buffalo. The chief leaned over and put the talisman around Aajim's neck.

"This will keep you safe on your journey—at least from my people. It means safe passage.

"May you live long and well. And may your story

comfort your people and make them proud."

The road home, thought Aajim, will be much more difficult than the road to the gathering. Even though I'm able to walk this trail, I'm pulling a heavy load.

He shared the trail with a few others who were returning home. Families carried their belongings and dragged them on poles lashed together, two legs leaving parallel trails—the same sort of conveyance on which he pulled his brother.

The children scrambled up and down the hillsides playing tag.

Some of the Dakota looked at him with curiosity. But all knew he was being allowed to go back to his band with Buffalo's blessings. At one point several older boys approached him, obviously looking for trouble. Aajim didn't understand what they were saying, but it was clear he was being taunted. One boy made the sign for "coward" by pointing at him and signing, "afraid."

Aajim countered with the signs for "no" and "afraid." The boy laughed derisively. Suddenly enraged, Aajim dropped his brother, pulled the ax from his belt and advanced on the weaponless boys. Seeing the expression on his face, they backed off. Before the situation could escalate, a man left his family and walked over shouting something at the young Dakota. They turned and walked on.

The man waited until Aajim slipped the ax back

in his belt. He stared at him without expression and then returned to his family.

––––––––––

The day wore on. Cold had returned. Gray clouds scudded quickly underneath a threatening sky. He hoped there would be no more rain.

The poles had already begun cutting into his palms. He cut pieces of hide and wrapped his hands. His neck and shoulders were aching from the strain of pulling Animikil over the rough, rutted trail.

Aajim realized that, for some reason, he had not yet thought of Minochige. He knew there was a chance he could fulfill his promise, but he was numb from all that had happened.

I just escaped death. How much more risk can I take? Is not the burden of my brother enough?

He walked a short distance off the trail to eat and drink at a stream. The swiftly flowing waters reminded him of his meeting with Minochige; reminded him that Giniw must have led him to her for a reason.

He heard his small voice again. "You will rescue Minochige."

But how?

Have her captors returned? Have they told her of the contests; of the 10 Anishinaabe who died and the youngest who was required to live? Would she wonder if he were coming for her?

And if I do, how will the two of us escape? The

camp is very open. I can't hide where I did, especially not in daylight. There will be people, dogs. If I come at night, how could I find her? Would she be ready and waiting for me? And Animikil would slow us down. She could help pull, but I wonder if her leg could take the strain.

As he walked on, he tried to think of a plan, but nothing seemed possible.

Tiredness descended on him like a blanket. As darkness began to cloak the trail, he walked into the grass, cut some clumps for bedding. He pulled Animikil next to him, ate and then collapsed, head on his pack.

The night was long and uncomfortable. Initially his dreams were fractured, meaningless.

Then he dreamed that Animikil rose from his hide wrappings and stood before him. Flowering Moon had risen and shown through his ghostly image.

"*Thank you, little brother, for taking me home. I'm sorry for the pain it is causing you. It will be good to be buried next to our sister so I can begin my journey. Now I am in darkness, waiting. And you will take Minochige with you. She will become an important part of your life. You are strong. And I know you will take care of our family.*"

Aajim tried to speak, but couldn't. His mouth wouldn't form the words in his mind. Goodbye, brother, he thought. Some day we will meet again. He watched as Animikil's form floated down slowly, melting back into his wrappings.

Near morning he dreamed of the three eagle feathers Minochige had given him, the ones he now carried in his pack. He awoke with the dream still fresh in his mind. He wondered if Giniw were responsible for it. If so, what could be its meaning? And Animikil? He foretold that he would rescue the girl.

Returning to the trail, Aajim couldn't get the dream of the feathers out of his head. Could he use them in a rescue attempt? What possible use could they be? Then he realized they were the one thing he and Minochige had in common; the one thing she would recognize as his.

What if I left Animikil in the undergrowth, snuck into camp tonight and stuck the feathers in the ground in front of her teepee? She must have early morning chores. She would know I'm there, somewhere, hiding and watching for her.

Aajim thought: It's not a great plan. But it might work.

———

Aajim now walked in a rhythm, his feet moving mechanically, his mind blank. He tried not to think of the burning sensation in his shoulders and legs; the blisters on his palms.

He sensed he was nearing Minochige's camp, but the almost featureless prairie looked utterly unfamiliar since he was approaching from the other direction.

"Aajim." He heard his name spoken clearly but quietly. He stopped and looked around. The trail was empty in both directions.

"Aajim!" More urgently.

The voice seemed to be coming from his right from a clump of bushes. He looked carefully and saw someone crouching and gesturing for him to come. It was Minochige. She darted back into the undergrowth.

He checked again. No sign of travelers. He pulled Animikil off the trail, laid him down, and found her hiding in the brambles.

She stood and looked at him shyly. Both started to talk at once. Aajim let her speak.

"They say you live. Not know if you come. I come for you. Sorry about brother, friends," she said haltingly.

She had obviously been working to remember their native tongue.

In response to his questioning look, "Leave before sun. They think I go forest."

"I'm glad to see you. I was coming, but did not know how to steal you back."

She smiled. "I bring food." She gestured to a pack.

"We must avoid trails," he said. "We still have a few hours left before dark. We will travel around your camp," he gestured, "and then into the forest."

"You bring brother. Will be hard."

"Yes, but we have no choice. I will take you *both* home."

———————

They walked until light had completely deserted

the land. Pulling Animikil over the rough and hummocky ground was exhausting. They couldn't go as fast as he would have liked. And the two-legged platform was leaving very visible dual tracks in the soft ground. Tomorrow, he thought, we must find a stream in which to travel to hide our tracks.

As they walked, Aajim considered the chance Minochige had taken in fleeing the camp and coming to look for him on the prairie. It was a brave thing to do, but could have had disastrous results if they had not found each other.

The moon was not yet up to help guide their way, so they found a place to bed down. The ground was still wet from the previous night's rain.

"Even if we had dry fuel," he said, "a fire would not be a good idea."

They ate and lay down to try to sleep. He ached, but his hands were the most painful. Nothing could be done.

It was cold; colder as the night wore on.

"Are you asleep?" he asked quietly. She said not. Aajim remembered how his parents lay close together on cold nights. He moved his pack next to her, lay on his side and took her in his arms. She was shivering. Gradually the tremors subsided. He was intrigued by the smell of her hair, the feeling of her form molded to his. Soon they slept.

———

In the morning they walked toward a hazy sun rising over the prairie. The sun had a faint ring around it. Its light seemed weak, diffused. Aajim could not remember ever seeing anything quite like this. He didn't like it.

It took a while for them to walk out the stiffness in their limbs. It felt good to be moving, generating body heat. Before leaving he cut and wrapped additional hide around his hands to provide more cushioning. The palms were not a pretty sight. Blisters had broken revealing raw flesh beneath.

Minochige offered to help. Each took one side, but it was slower and more awkward with two than one.

"I pull?" she asked. She took over for a short while, but it was obvious the load was too much for her. It might have been different over a trail. But the rough and uneven ground made it difficult. And there was the constant need to avoid obstacles.

Looking at her leg: "Hurt?"

She nodded, looking apologetic.

"I will pull," he said.

They made their way as best they could through the jumbled terrain—marshes, streams, ponds, tall grasses, fields of large boulders—stopping often for Aajim to catch his breath.

For part of the time, they waded in the almost freezing waters of a stream that headed primarily east—their direction. Pulling his brother through the mostly muddy stream bottom wasn't much easier, but at least they weren't leaving any tracks. Several times he stopped, unwrapped his hands, and soaked them in the icy water to provide some relief.

After walking until about mid-afternoon, he felt it was safe to head northeast, toward the forest, Gichigami and his village.

The two stopped to rest and ate dried fish, nuts and berries.

Minochige looked at him. She had something to say, but seemed reluctant.

"Why make war? Can't win. All kill but you."

Aajim looked away, staring at the hazy horizon. Yes, why he wondered. Her question sounded like the one asked by Buffalo.

"Honor," he said.

"Honor?" She shook her head and looked away. "Women not know honor," she said. "Women make life, give life. Men take life away. For honor?"

They walked on. It was getting colder. Their breath became frosty. The sun had given up and was shrouded in increasingly thick cloud cover. The wind, Aajim sensed, had shifted and was coming from the east. He didn't know much about weather, but he did know that the east wind usually brought rain or snow.

By mid-afternoon they entered an area of transition, a scattering of pines that thickened as they went. Soon tall trees formed a welcomed canopy overhead.

Minochige seemed entranced by the change in terrain. Aajim could see that memories of her former life in the forest were returning. But he worried about the weather. The wind had picked up. It carried the smell the rain, or was it snow. Spring blizzards were not uncommon.

Soon his fears were realized. A few tentative flakes. They were large and wet. With their every step, the snow seemed to intensify. The wind began to whip the flakes into a frenzy and howl through the tree tops, creating an eerie keening.

"We must find shelter!" But where?

He could think of only one thing. As they walked as quickly as they could into the gathering gloom, Aajim looked left and right, hoping to find what he sought.

Snow already covered the ground when he did. An old, tall spruce with large dead branches around its base. He led her to the tree. Minochige was mystified until Aajim drew his ax and crawled under it. The quarters were cramped, but, in the failing light, he hacked away at several branches. She understood and pulled them free once they were cut.

Soon there was a small cave under the tree. They crawled in, and like *misakakojiish*, badger, scooped pine needles and soil out through their legs to deepen the hole. He pulled Animikil as close to the entrance as he could, hoping his body would help shield them from the storm. The cut branches were used to cover the entrance. When ready, they would insulate themselves with the mixture of pine needles and soil.

They pushed their packs up against the trunk. Aajim had left his weapons, except for the ax, outside in the ever-deepening snow.

"I don't know if I can get a fire started, but the branches around us are dry. We can use them as fuel."

He rummaged around in his pack and found the small fire-starter pouch. With numb fingers, he was able to withdraw the two fire stones and dry, pithy kindling. He then reached overhead and stripped highly flammable needles from the branches. Minochige began snapping off twigs and small branches.

Now, remembering his game, he began to strike. He counted. *Bezhig, niizh, niswi....* On the third strike a small flame blossomed. Good, he thought. But why am I still playing this child's game?

Carefully fed, a small fire flickered, lighting their little cave. Its smoke drifted up through the branches.

"We must keep it small. We don't want to catch our new home on fire," he said. Minochige smiled. "I don't know if it will keep us very warm, but a fire is always good for the spirit."

They collected twigs and branches to keep the fire going as long as they could.

Though still cold, they felt safe under this venerable tree. The wind howled and the entrance to the tree-cave and Animikil were quickly covered with blowing and drifting snow. They felt the tree's big trunk sway slightly in the gale.

Aajim said a brief prayer to Gichi-Manidoo to thank Him for the shelter and ask that the storm be brief.

They ate, curled up on either side of the fire and

spread as much of the earthy mixture as they could over their bodies.

"We freeze?" Minochige asked.

"Depends how long the storm lasts. But, if we have food and shelter, I think we'll survive."

Cold, exhausted, they slept and fed the fire during short periods of wakefulness.

———

Aajim awoke, disoriented. It took a moment for him to remember where he was. He moved. Though cold, all his limbs seemed to be working. The fire was out. He looked at Minochige. Her face was peaceful. He prayed she was alive. He reached over and shook her shoulder. Slowly her eyes opened. At first they seemed unfocused. Then she moved; a slight smile on her lips.

"We alive," she said simply.

All was very quiet. No wind. A soft light filtered into the tree-cave from above. The storm had passed.

"Let's rebuild the fire, warm ourselves and eat. Then we can crawl out of our burrow and see how much snow we must contend with."

Chapter 17

Homecoming

They moved the branches away from the tree-cave opening and crawled like misakakojiish from their burrow. Snow had drifted around Animikil, helping to insulate the small cave.

Limbs stiff, they stood slowly, shedding the pine needle and soil blanket that helped keep them warm.

All was white. Warm sunlight filtered through snow-laden boughs. Icicles were forming, some already as long as Aajim's forearm. They dripped, pattering on the snow beneath. Some caught the sun and glistened, bright against the dark foliage.

Generally, the snow wasn't too deep. The strong wind had scoured some areas clean, piling snow against downed trees and clumps of ferns.

They pulled their packs out of the burrow and Aajim rummaged through the snow to retrieve his weapons.

Minochige looked at the tree, gazing upward at its crown.

"I will call my first girl child 'Spruce.'"

"The first thing we must do is find moss for our moccasins," Aajim said. He knew the thick leather would help keep their feet dry, but would not keep them warm.

They walked from pine tree to pine tree, scraping moss from their trunks where they found it. When they'd gathered an armful, they sat on a boulder, pulled off their moccasins and quickly stuffed them with as much moss as they could and still leave room for their feet.

Moccasins insulated, the two resumed their journey northeast. Deer had been out browsing after the storm. He smelled their scat and soon found an active trail heading more-or-less in the right direction. The snow-covered trail made it easier to pull his brother for a while until the trail veered southeast.

They trudged on.

———

Aajim wondered about the homecoming. He thought: I can't just suddenly walk into camp. Once I was seen, there would be great confusion. People would come running to learn what had happened to the others. He couldn't imagine facing their families like that.

I think I'd better wait until close to dark and try to sneak with Minochige into our wigwam. There I would tell my family what had happened, and father could arrange a meeting with the entire band the next day. Then I could tell everyone at once.

The thought of standing before The People to tell

the story made him feel sick. The knot again was forming in his gut.

––––––––––

Sometime after mid-day, they came upon a stream flowing north. Aajim couldn't tell for certain, but he suspected it was the stream he followed when tracking the boys. They turned to follow its meandering course through the forest.

He again stopped several times to soak his hands, hoping the nearly freezing water would relieve some of the pain.

Aajim told Minochige of his plan. She nodded.

"Family like me?" she asked. "Where I live?"

He stopped, realizing he hadn't thought about this.

"Yes, they will like you. And you will live with us."

The answer seemed to satisfy her. But not him.

Who is this girl? What is she to be to me? An adopted sister? Why did Giniw bring us together?

He considered how he felt about her and realized it wasn't the same feeling he had for his sisters.

"Is Minochige to be my wife?" he muttered almost to himself.

She looked at him quizzically, wondering what he had mumbled.

––––––––––

The forest was darkening when they came upon Gichigami.

She gasped with surprise at the enormous watery

vista that spread before them. She looked at him.

"Great Water?"

Aajim smiled. "Yes, we are nearly home."

The rocky beach was icy following the blizzard. They had to watch their footing. The pounding waves of the storm had left behind many large puddles that were now frozen. They provided a welcomed slippery surface over which Aajim could drag his brother's remains. Soon they passed the huge rocks hugging the shoreline, the stunted white cedar atop the split boulder silhouetted black against the setting sun.

Aajim wondered how best to enter the camp. He led Minochige past bench rock and then some distance down the beach and up a little used trail that ran alongside the camp. The sun was gone and the cold had descended with it. But they had to wait until it was dark enough to cloak their entry.

———

When Aajim could barely see, they rose from their hiding place and moved quietly into camp. He left Animikil's body behind the tree line. The family's evening cooking fire had burned to glowing embers. It cast a dim, orange light on the walls of the wigwam.

It appeared his family was inside, preparing to settle for the night. Their figures were shadows on the walls cast by the light of a small fire.

He approached the door flap. Quietly: "Father, Mother—it's Aajim." There was stirring followed by muffled voices. From the other side of the flap: "Aajim, is that you?" It was his father.

"Yes."

The flap flew open. His father stood in the doorway, naked from the waist up. He looked at Aajim with disbelief and then gathered him in his arms. His mother joined them.

"Animikil?" she asked. He shook his head. She slumped into his father's arms and began weeping.

"Quickly, come in. We were sure we lost you *both*."

Aajim signaled for Minochige to join them. Shyly, she stepped into the dim light.

"This is Minochige," he said. "She's with me."

Once inside: "There are many questions," said his father. "But you must be cold, hungry and tired. Come, sit by the fire." He added more wood. His mother, struggling to regain her composure, said, "We can reheat the evening meal."

Aajim knelt so his sisters, in their sleeping robes, could throw their arms around him.

"Where have you been?" asked *Oniijaaniw*, Doe, oldest of the two. "Where is Animikil? And who is this?" pointing to Minochige.

"Hush. Enough questions. Let your brother sit."

The meal was soon ready, their first hot food in days. Aajim found himself eating quickly, not as much from hunger, but to be able to answer questions that swirled unspoken around the fire.

He began: "I was not part of the raiding party led by Keeshagkoni. Animikil told me I couldn't come.

But I followed them...."

Aajim told the story for the first time, but without much detail. He did, though, talk at length about Animikil, how he became the group's leader, how he killed the son of the Dakota war party's leader—with the taunting spear.

"And," he said, "I brought his body back. He is just outside."

"How did you...?" his father stopped. "That explains your hands," he said.

"Minochige helped and I ask that she be welcomed into our wigwam. Unless by some miracle her family or band can be found, she has nowhere else to go."

"Of course she's welcome," said his mother.

His father said, "We searched for you. We did find Keeshagkoni and Inaabiwin and brought them back. All signs indicated the rest had been captured and taken. Our small search party could not follow into Dakota Territory.

"Many, especially those who lost sons, wanted to enlist the aid of other bands and mount a war party. Others said we could never find the boys and, even if we did, it would be too late. Sadly, your story ends the argument.

"I will call the band together in the morning so all can hear what happened."

Minochige was given a beaver-pelt blanket. She would sleep in Animikil's place next to Aajim.

"Family nice," she said quietly as she nestled

under the blanket. "I like here."

They talked for a few minutes until sleep overcame them.

Mikinaak rose early and slipped out of the dwelling. He went from family to family to let them know Aajim had returned with news of the missing boys. Once he completed his rounds, he built a large fire in the central clearing. Soon the people began arriving in small groups from all corners of the camp.

Meanwhile Aajim gathered the medicine bags of the fallen boys and put them in his pack. He knew to whom many had belonged, but some he didn't recognize. He would have to let those families identify their sons' bags.

He looked at Minochige.

"I not go. No one know me."

"I want you there," he said simply. He felt that, somehow, her presence would give him courage.

His mother and sisters went to join Mikinaak. Aajim and Minochige followed. Tentatively, Aajim took her hand. She had braided her lustrous black hair and tried to hide her limp as they approached the gathering.

On seeing Aajim, restlessness ran through the crowd. Those in back struggled to see. Minochige looked at him, smiled with encouragement, and walked to join his family.

He opened his pack, knelt and nervously spread

11 medicine bags in the fresh snow at his feet. Some were bloodstained. They were all that remained of his friends, all he had to offer their families. All, except their story.

As he rose, a shadow suddenly skittered along the ground. He looked up and saw the silhouette of Giniw as he crossed the sun. The eagle screamed, wheeled and circled the clearing. All looked skyward.

Giniw's presence gave him courage. He knew the first thing he had to say: "All are dead."

He was surprised that his voice was strong and without quaver. Although everyone must have expected that would be the message, many mothers began to wail.

Aajim waited.

When the expressions of grief subsided, he told the story of the 13 boys who sought revenge; who sought to restore the honor of the band. Despite his youth, the words came easily. He found a rhythm. The story flowed unbroken and with power.

The crowd was mesmerized as he talked of following the war party, of finding Keeshagkoni and Inaabiwin, of his help from Giniw, of White Buffalo's offer and the contests that followed, of the bravery of their sons and brothers, of his struggle to return Animikil, of the rescue of Minochige and their survival in the blizzard....

He talked until the fire had burned to embers.

When he finished, there was an eerie silence broken only by the gentle whisper of wind through the tops of the pines. He felt as if he were awakening from a dream, a trance. He realized his feet were cold from standing so long in the thin layer of snow. He felt empty. It was as if telling the story had drained him of all feeling—except loneliness.

Before families of the slain boys could approach to claim spirit bundles, the shaman, father of Innabiwin, stepped forward. He faced Aajim and put a hand on his shoulder.

Quietly: "You have done well. Sometimes living is more difficult than dying. Your burden is to carry your friends in your heart and make them live again whenever you tell the story. The mystery of your name has been revealed. This is the story it foretold."

Innabam turned to face the families. He looked up, raised both hands and prayed to Gichi-Manidoo to speed the journey of the boys along the Road of Souls and to accept them with honor in The Home After Death.

Aajim scanned the crowd, found the face of Minochige, and felt his loneliness begin to melt with the early spring snow.

Epilogue

Debwe joined the rag-tag herd of boys heading for the beach. It was mid-morning. The day was glorious—sky deep blue; sun warm. Biboon was waning and the boys, cooped up much of the winter, had energy to burn.

Play, however, was never just play. The boys were admonished to be on the lookout for driftwood and seagull eggs to supplement the diminished food supply.

Debwe was nearly 13, a little older than the rest of the group that raced up and down the twisting trail to see who could be first to hit the beach. He lagged, knowing he could outrun them if he wanted to. He didn't. He was content to reacquaint himself with the gradually reappearing scenery hidden in snow and ice for many months and to look for signs of animals just awakened from their winter's sleep.

By the time he reached the beach, the boys had scattered. He looked down the rocky shore and saw Akiwenzil still sitting on bench rock. Odd, he thought, that the old man was still on the beach with the black dog. Debwe had joined him briefly early that morning. He usually returned in time for the morning meal. The dog was with him now but had been in camp earlier.

Debwe and the old man had a special relationship. To him he wasn't just an ancient grandfather who could barely walk, see or hear. He was Aajim, teller of the story of the 13, a story he had heard him tell many times in his young life. He knew the story by heart and he and Aajim had talked about it. During some winter evenings, he had been a guest in his wigwam and felt privileged to learn more about his long life and ask questions about the story.

As he approached Akiwenzil he sensed something was wrong. The dog stood, bared his fangs and growled menacingly. He stopped, surprised by the dog's strange behavior. He waited. Soon the animal's aggression abated. He sat and began to whimper.

Throughout this display, the old man didn't move. The boy came closer and saw his chin resting on his chest.

"No!" Debwe said. He hurried to the ancient one and gently shook his shoulder, hoping he was merely asleep. But Akiwenzil slumped and began to fall over. He grabbed him by the shoulders and, not knowing what else to do, laid him on the rock.

He didn't want to leave him. He shouted down the beach at a knot of boys. Sensing something was happening, they came running.

"He's dead. Go to camp and get help."

Wide eyed, they scampered off.

The black dog lay down at the base of the rock, his head resting on his paws.

He sat at the old man's feet and looked at his face. It was peaceful, younger looking. Gone were the lines of pain that frequently creased it as he struggled to make his old body do things it could no longer do.

He remembered the last time they talked about the story. Instead of asking the questions, Akiwenzil, for some reason, had asked questions of him. It was almost if he were testing him on his memory of story details.

"And who were the boys?" he had asked. Debwe easily listed them all and included descriptions of his favorites: Animikil, his brother; Makwa, his friend; and the twins who died as they lived—together.

"Tell me about Minochige."

"Giniw led you to her. You stole her back from the Dakota and she became your wife."

"What happened to the taunting spear?"

"Animikil used it to slay the son of the leader of the raiding party. It is buried here with him to be carried to The Home After Death."

"And why did the 13 make war on the Dakota?"

"For revenge. To regain the honor of our band."

Akiwenzil had looked away and was quiet. When he looked again at Debwe, his expression had changed. But it was unreadable.

"And did we? Did we restore honor to the band?"

He thought. They had never discussed this before.

The times he had heard Aajim tell the story, he couldn't remember him raising or being asked this question.

"Yes," he said.

"Don't be so certain, young Debwe. I have struggled with this question all my long life. I'm afraid I will die not knowing the answer."

"I know all but *you* died," Debwe interjected. "But don't you believe that—as Keeshagkoni and Animikil said—in matters of honor, it's the attempt that counts, not what happens."

"You listened and remember well," he said. "But I have come to believe there is more honor in living than dying. There is honor in living well, in raising and caring for a family, in helping the band survive and prosper. There is no honor in revenge. Revenge leads to more revenge, to more and more death. Where is the honor in that?"

Then he said something even stranger.

"In years to come, when you tell the story of the 13, remember what I have said."

That was the last time they had spoken of the story.

Soon men came from the village. As they lifted Akiwenzil, one commented that he weighed little more than a handful of feathers.

The boy and the dog followed the small procession.

He was buried the following day next to his beloved Minochige. She had died in childbirth early in their marriage. The tiny girl child survived and was named

Gaawaandag, Spruce, as her mother had instructed.

She grew up straight and tall and beautiful like her namesake. Aajim was heartbroken when, as must happen, she married a young man from a distant band. He saw Gaawaandag and his grandchildren only rarely and, as his life stretched on, outlived her, his only child.

Debwe was among the many who attended his burial.

The large flowering tree which overspread the burial ground also covered the graves of his parents and brother. He knew it grew from the grave of Aajim's sister who had died so many years ago. The tree was coming into bloom. Soon it would be covered with pink and white blossoms that would later flutter to the ground, blanketing the graves.

Concluding his tribute to Aajim, the shaman said, "Our loss is great, for who will tell the story of the 13 now that Aajim is gone?"

He looked directly at Debwe and smiled.

He knows, he thought. The boy stepped forward.

"I will," he said.

Afterword

The idea for the story of *The 13* was not mine. It came years ago from historian Dr. Walker Wyman, a fellow faculty member and friend at the University of Wisconsin—River Falls. Walker, who was known primarily as a folklorist, published 23 books during his long career. In 1979, following publication of his *Wisconsin Folklore*, he was named Wisconsin's "Honorary Folklorist" by Gov. Lee Dreyfus.

Walker told me the Ojibwe tale sometime in the early 1980s during a faculty cocktail party at his home. It was my habit to avoid such gatherings whenever possible, but this, fortunately, was an exception. At the time one of my responsibilities was serving as the university's director of outreach and I was working with Walker to develop a "newspaper classroom" course about Wisconsin folklore. We were discussing possible course content over drinks when he mentioned an Ojibwe story he'd recently heard. He had only the sketchiest of details and I assumed he might, through research, later fill in the blanks.

Try as I might, I can't remember whether he called it a legend or merely a story. But I do remember I was intrigued by the tale of 13 boys who, after a devastating raid on their village by the Dakota/ Sioux, sought to restore the honor of their band through revenge—in defiance of their elders—with tragic results. The journalist in me thought—there are ingredients here for a great story. So, I filed it away in my mental compartment labeled "Ideas for Novels" that I hoped someday to write.

Walker and I never again discussed the story. He died at age 91 in 1999. It was some 33 years after that cocktail party that I started to write *The 13*. I've found no trace of the story in his academic output written after our conversation—books, articles and other materials—that are stored in the university's archive.

So *The 13* is my creation, built on the meagre details Walker provided. I hope readers will agree that, whether legend or story, the tale was one worth the telling.

Acknowledgements

Many resources were helpful in filling in the historical and cultural details necessary to bring the story to life. These included:

- *A Concise Dictionary of Minnesota Ojibwe*, John D. Nichols and Earl Nyholm (1995)

- *Cheryl Jimenez, member, Mississippi Band of Ojibwe, White Earth, MN*

- *History of the Ojibway People*, William W. Warren (1885)

- *Kitchi-Gami: Life Among the Lake Superior Ojibway*, Johann Georg Kohl (1860)

- *Living Our Language: Ojibwe Tales and Oral Histories*, Dr. Anton Treuer (2010)

- *Narrative journal of travels through the northwestern regions of the United States, extending from Detroit through the great chain of American lakes to .... the Mississippi River, in the year 1820,* Henry Rowe Schoolcraft, author; Mentor L. Williams, editor (1953)

- *Ojibway Ceremonies,* Basil Johnston (1982)

- *Ojibway Heritage,* Basil Johnston (1976)

- *The Manitous: The Supernatural World of the Ojibway,* Basil Johnston (1995)